P

CHILDISH LITERATURE

ALEJANDRO ZAMBRA was born in Santiago, Chile, in 1975. He is the author of *Chilean Poet*, *Multiple Choice*, *Not to Read*, *My Documents*, *Ways of Going Home*, *The Private Lives of Trees*, and *Bonsai*. In Chile, among other honors, he has won the National Book Council Award for best novel three times. In English, he has won the English PEN Award and the PEN/O. Henry Prize and was a finalist for the Frank O'Connor International Short Story Award. In 2023, he won the Manuel Rojas Ibero-American Narrative Award for the totality of his oeuvre. He has also won the Prince Claus Award (Holland) and received a Cullman Center Fellowship from the New York Public Library. His books have been translated into twenty languages, and his stories have been published in *The New Yorker*, *The New York Times Magazine*, *The Paris Review*, *Granta*, *McSweeney's Quarterly*, and *Harper's Magazine*, among other publications. He has taught creative writing and Hispanic literature for fifteen years and currently lives in Mexico City.

MEGAN MCDOWELL's translations have won the National Book Award, the English PEN Award, the Premio Valle-Inclán, the Shirley Jackson Award, and two O. Henry Prizes, among others, and have been nominated for the International Booker Prize four times. In 2020, she won an American Academy of Arts and Letters Award in Literature. She lives in Santiago, Chile.

Childish Literature

Alejandro Zambra

TRANSLATED BY

Megan McDowell

PENGUIN BOOKS

PENGUIN BOOKS
An imprint of Penguin Random House LLC
penguinrandomhouse.com

Originally published in Spanish as *Literatura infantil*
by Editorial Anagrama, Barcelona.

The following translated works were originally published in different forms:
"Trip and Crawl (Teonanácatl Blues)" (as "Teonanácatl") in *The Paris Review*;
"Crowd" (as "Multitude") in *The New York Review of Books*; "Screen Time" in
The New York Times Magazine; "Childhood's Childhood" (as "What Will
My Son Remember of This Horrible Year?") in *The New York Times Magazine*;
"Skyscrapers" in *The New Yorker*; "An Introduction to Soccer Sadness" in
McSweeney's; and "Blue-Eyed Muggers" in *Granta*.

LIBRARY OF CONGRESS CATALOGING-IN-PUBLICATION DATA
Names: Zambra, Alejandro, 1975– author. | McDowell, Megan, translator.
Title: Childish Literature / Alejandro Zambra ; translated by Megan McDowell.
Other titles: Literatura infantil. English
Description: New York : Penguin Books, 2024.
Identifiers: LCCN 2024017613 (print) | LCCN 2024017614 (ebook) |
ISBN 9780143138082 (paperback) | ISBN 9780593512173 (ebook)
Subjects: LCSH: Zambra, Alejandro, 1975—Translations
into English. | LCGFT: Short stories. | Essays. | Poetry.
Classification: LCC PQ8098.36.A43 L5813 2024 (print) |
LCC PQ8098.36.A43 (ebook) | DDC 863/.64—dc23/eng/20240503
LC record available at https://lccn.loc.gov/2024017613
LC ebook record available at https://lccn.loc.gov/2024017614

Printed in the United States of America
1st Printing

Set in Adobe Caslon Pro

For Silvestre's mom

and Jazmina's son

Ever since my childhood, I have liked to have a bird's-eye view of my room.

—BRUNO SCHULZ

We aren't born writers, we're born babies.

—HEBE UHART

Contents

I.

Childish Literature

0

With you in my arms, I see the shadow we cast together on the wall for the first time. You've been alive for twenty minutes.

Your mother's eyelids lower, but she doesn't want to sleep. She rests her eyes for just a few seconds.

"Sometimes newborns forget to breathe," a friendly buzz-kill of a nurse informs us.

I wonder if she says it like that every day. With the same words. With the same sad cautionary tone.

Your little body breathes, though: even in the dimly lit hospital, your breathing is visible. But I want to hear it, hear you, and my own wheezing breath won't let me. And my noisy heart keeps me from hearing yours.

Throughout the night, every two or three minutes I hold my breath to make sure you're breathing. It's such a reasonable superstition, the most reasonable of all: stop breathing so your child will breathe.

1

I walk through the hospital as though searching for cracks left by the last earthquake. I think horrible thoughts, but I still manage to imagine the scars that someday you will proudly show off toward the end of summer.

14

Your brief fourteen-day life wears the word *childhood* like a roomy poncho. But I like how exaggerated it sounds. Fourteen days old—the word *old* looks so strange there, when you're still so relentlessly new.

25

You cry and I show up. What a rip-off. Maybe our fathers took those first rejections too much to heart.

You don't prefer me, but you get used to my company. And I get used to sleeping when you sleep. The rhythm of intermittent naps reminds me of hundreds of long bus rides dozing on the way to grade school or university, to attend classes where I went right on dozing off. Or those delicious, furtive catnaps that allowed me to endure a working life.

Suddenly, I'm fifteen years old and it's midnight and I'm studying something that might be chemistry or algebra or phonology and I'm out of cigarettes and it's a problem, because I smoke a lot in my dreams. I wake up when some shy dogs start their concert of barks and a neighbor starts hammering; perhaps he's hanging a portrait of his own son on the wall, and that's why he doesn't care about waking mine.

But you go on sleeping against my chest, and you seem to be even more deeply asleep, seriously asleep. I have no idea what time it is, and I don't care. Eleven in the morning, three in the afternoon. That's how the tired but happy days pass, alternating with the happy but tired days and the happy but happy days.

31

The birth of a child heralds a far-reaching future in which we will not fully participate. Julio Ramón Ribeyro summed it up well: "The tooth that comes in for them is the one that falls out for us; the inch they grow is the one that we shrink; the lights they acquire are the ones extinguished in us; what they learn, we forget; and the year added for them is the one subtracted for us."

It's a beautiful thought, whose turbulent side, however, has unhinged millions of men. I'm thinking of fathers from past generations, though it's ridiculous to presume things have changed. I have met men who practice fatherhood with lucidity, humor, and humility, but I have also seen dear friends who seemed to have their hearts well placed turn away from their children to indulge in a desperate and clichéd recovery of their youth. And there are also plenty of fathers who confront the death drive by burdening their kids with missions and commandments, with the explicit or veiled intention of using their children to further their own interrupted dreams.

What I find striking, in any case, is the almost absolute lack of a tradition. Since all human beings—I assume—have been born, it would seem natural for us to be experts in matters of child-rearing, but it turns out that we know very little, especially men, who sometimes seem like those cheerful students who show up to class blissfully unaware that there's a test. While women passed on to their daughters the asphyxiating imperative of maternity, we grew up pampered and ineffectual and even humming along to "Billie Jean." Our fathers tried, in their own ways, to teach us to be men, but they never taught us to be fathers. And their fathers didn't teach them either. And so on.

42

During your first weeks of life I have written around a hundred poems on my phone. They're not poems, really, but on the phone it's easier to press Enter than to struggle with punctuation.

I write in a state of attachment, under your influence, both of us inveigled by the spell of the rocking chair, which functions like a bashful roller coaster, or like a tireless, generous horse, or like the ferry that will eventually carry us to Staten Island—or, even better, to Chiloé.

49

This morning I tried to turn the fake poems into real poems, but I'm afraid I overshot and ended up guiding them toward the civilized and legible country of prose. I ruined them, but I still copied them all, just in case, into a file that I titled "Children's Literature." None of those sketches could be considered children's literature, though all of them deal with childhood. Yours, incipient, and mine, long gone. My childhood or my idea of childhood since you arrived.

50

The word *childish* is often used as an insult, although the words that aren't insults but can fulfill the function of one are almost infinite. You just have to work on the tone a little.

I remember a very sweet little girl, the daughter of one of my best friends, who one day got angry with her favorite stuffed animal and spent about two hours yelling at it cruelly, over and over: "A *toy!* That's all you are, a toy! You think you're real, but you're just a toy, that's all!"

When I was fifteen it annoyed me when people referred to me using the phrase *young man*. I don't remember if I was ever called a *teenager* to my face, but I would have hated it. In the strict plane of language, *teenager* is a perfectly accurate word, but *adolescent* is much more evocative.

61

Literature has ceded to self-help nearly all the reflective space that fatherhood requires. But self-help books usually hold nothing but hackneyed and at times even humiliating advice. A few months ago, I read a voluminous manual whose brilliant recommendation for men was this: "Be sensitive!"

62

This week you gained the same four ounces that I must have lost dancing with you in my arms. The son gains the weight that his father sheds. It's the perfect diet.

83

The expression *children's literature* is condescending and offensive and also strikes me as redundant, because all literature, at its core, is childish. Much as we try to hide it, those of us who write do so because we want to recover perceptions that were erased by the ostensible learning that so often made us unhappy. Enrique Lihn said that we surrender to our real age as though under false evidence.

Children's literature: I like what the word *childhood* awakens by lurking behind those words. It makes me think of Jorge Teillier, Hebe Uhart, Bruno Schulz, Gabriela Mistral, Jacques Prévert. Well, the list of "children's authors" is endless. Baudelaire defined literature as a "childhood recovered at will"—I just checked this, and found that it was actually artistic "genius" that he defined that way, not literature.

Still, I'd rather stick with my recollection, wrong but less pompous, of Baudelaire's theory—I prefer that emphasis. I like, above all, how Baudelaire compares the artist and child with a convalescent. More than remembering or relating, a writer is trying to see things *as though for the first time*. That is, like a child, or like a convalescent on their way back from illness and in a way from death, and who has to relearn, for example, how to walk.

Parenthood is another kind of convalescence that allows us to learn everything again. And we didn't even know we had been gravely ill. We've only just found out.

96

Stepfathers start from behind in the noisy battle of legitimacy. But then someone comes along and says, "My stepfather was my real father." Those are the stories I want to hear.

Perhaps all fathers are, in a way, stepfathers to our children. Biology assures us a place in their lives, but we still long to be chosen. For our children to someday say these wonderfully strange words: *My father was my real father.*

101

On the way back from the bakery we go to every morning, a man says to me:

"Doesn't that kid have a mom?"

"Asshole. Asshole," I reply.

I used to be good at comebacks, but I can only come up with that one word. The same insult, twice.

The man is more or less my age, with a fancy suit and dry green eyes. He doesn't seem drunk.

For a second, I think about asking him to wait while I put you in your crib at home and come right back to punch his lights out. It bothers me so much to have a thought like that. It makes me sad, rather. Demoralizes me.

What kind of person would say such a thing? Why, what for?

I leave you in your mother's arms.

In the kitchen, I eat an entire baguette while thinking up crude, savage, definitive insults.

120

My father became a father at twenty-four years old, while I did at forty-two. I can't stop thinking about that. It is what it is.

When you have a child, you become someone's child again. But your own experience, tamed by time and shaped or channeled by idealization, discord, or absence, is not enough.

You would like to remember the days and nights when you were cared for the way you now care for your child. Though maybe you weren't cared for as much. Maybe they stuck you in the playpen and let you cry and stuffed a pacifier in your mouth. And turned on the TV, and that was that.

We compare ourselves to our fathers, even though—we know—we can no longer be the same as them or essentially different from them. And since we killed them when we were twenty, we can't kill them again now; for that very reason, sometimes we end up resurrecting them.

147

You cry when you realize that your feet are not meant for grabbing hold of objects. But then, astonished, you start interpreting the patterns on the sheets. And the imperfections in the quilt. And the raindrops on the window. Your mother imitates thunder and I imitate lightning. All is well.

158

There are men for whom fatherhood hits too hard. It's as if overnight, from the mere fact of becoming fathers, they lose the ability to utter a single sentence without going into a story starring their children, who, more than their children, seem like their spiritual leaders, because for these lovestruck dads, even the blandest anecdote possesses a certain philosophical depth. That is, exactly, my case.

I can imagine what a disaster it would have been for me to have a child when I was twenty. I belong to a generation that put off parenthood, or ruled it out entirely, or practiced it in other ways that were just as hard or harder, like adoption or stepparenthood—a word that, according to the Real Academia Española or *Merriam-Webster's* dictionary, does not exist, though the *Oxford English Dictionary* has incorporated it.

Now, at forty-two years old, paternity has been a real party for me. As we know, even the best parties have moments when the euphoria is mixed with unease or the unpleasant reminder that tomorrow we still have to get up early and wash the dishes. But if I had to summarize these hundred-plus days in a short sentence, my telegram would say: *I'm having a great time.*

203

"So, why did you want to have a child?"

In these few months, about fifteen people have allowed themselves to ask me this question.

"What I really want is to be a grandfather, this is just the first step," I might reply, for example.

Or maybe:

"Because I'm sick of cats."

"Because it was time."

"For personal reasons."

"Because I'm in love."

"Out of curiosity."

I particularly like this last answer, so graceful and banal. Maybe it would be better to talk about intellectual curiosity or an urge to experiment. Or to invoke the desire for adventure, the prestigious thirst for experience, or a need to understand human nature. But I like the simple, Pandora-style answer best.

After the jokes, though, I do answer, or at least I try to. I'm incapable of articulating a purely rational discourse, but if I just avoid the question with economical cynicism, I'll only add to the knowledge gap, so disheartening and disturbing, that we have all felt and suffered from.

209

For ages, literature has avoided sentimentalism like the plague. I have the impression that even today, many writers would rather be ignored than run the risk of being considered corny or mawkish. And the truth is that when it comes to writing about our children, happiness and tenderness defy our old masculine idea of the communicable. What to do, then, with the joyous and necessarily dopey satisfaction of watching a child learn to stand up or say his first words? And what kind of mirror is a child?

Literary tradition abounds with *letters to my father*, but *letters to my son* are pretty scarce. The reasons are predictable—sexism, selfishness, shame, adultcentrism, negligence, self-censorship—but maybe it would be worth adding some purely literary reasons, because those of us who have tried know that writing about your own children is quite an artistic challenge. Certainly, it's easier to omit kids or relegate them to the sidelines, or to see them as obstacles to writing and employ them as excuses; now it turns out it's all their fault we haven't been able to concentrate on our arduous, imposing novel.

Childhood lives on in us as an intermittent enigma, usually

only borne witness to by photo albums, "transitional" teddy bears, or handfuls of agates collected one day at the beach. No one wrote the story of our childhoods, and maybe we regret that lack of a record, but also, in a way, we are grateful for it, because it allows us to breathe, change, rebel. To imagine that our children will read our own work is, likewise, as exhilarating as it is overwhelming. To narrate the world that a child will forget—to become our children's correspondents—is an enormous challenge.

As I write, I myself feel the temptation of silence. And yet I know that even if I locked myself in to draft a novel about magnetic fields or to ad-lib an essay about the word *word*, I would end up talking about my son.

210

"Don't write about your dreams, please, and don't even think about mentioning children or pets," a prizewinning writer told a friend of mine who wanted to write a novel about her dreams and about her daughter and about her cat. I tend to think it would be better to take on every one of those challenges.

221

I'm proud to say that the first word my son uttered, five days ago, was, against all statistical probability, the word *dada*. Now he says it all the time. He still has trouble, though, articulating the voiceless bilabial plosive *d*, and for now he replaces it with the voiced bilabial nasal *m*.

226

Every person who has raised a child knows that there are many occasions when the word *happiness* inexplicably rhymes with *pain*, as in *lower back pain*.

235

"Zambra, when you guys come to Chile, I want to be the first to meet your son, even though you've never shown the slightest interest in meeting my kids."

That's what a dear Chilean friend says to me. It's a joke. It's true that I haven't met any of his three children, but the youngest of them has just turned forty. Besides, we talk about them all the time, and I keep up with what's going on in their lives. I know, for example, that the oldest didn't want to be a mother, and the younger two think becoming a father would be madness.

Suddenly I realize how meaningful those long conversations with my friend have been for me. And I thank him. "Laying it on a little thick, huh?" he replies.

"I don't want to die without being a grandfather," he tells me later.

"Laying it on a little thick, huh?" I reply.

247

Since I am not immune to optimism, I tend to think that, these days, we accept that even our own children don't belong to us and are destined to understand the world according to categories that we couldn't even conceive of. "Always at the door waiting for them without ever asking them to return," Massimo Recalcati says luminously in his stupendous book *The Son's Secret*.

251

I can hear "Praying for Time," George Michael's beautiful song, playing in the distance. I remember when I used to listen to that song and try to decipher its devastating lyrics using a tiny English–Spanish dictionary. I'm grateful to my neighbor for this involuntary trip back to turbulent youth. Now you are sleeping soundly to the beat of "Freedom!"

I don't ever complain about loud music. I'd rather start dancing. Or remembering. Or praying. I'm more inclined to complain about the noise of motorcycles, but they go by so fast.

I can't understand why anyone would complain about a child's crying. People who gripe about crying children should be grounded—no dessert, no TV, and no recess.

I was going to end it at the aphorism, but I want to leave a record of the lady who came over this morning to knock at the door because you'd been crying for two whole minutes. Three sharp blows with an open palm. What a fine person.

258

Our idea of upward mobility is a house with two bathrooms.

262

"You chose the wrong genre," an Italian editor told me once. We were speaking Spanish, which uses the same word for *genre* and for *gender*, so for a second I thought she was paying me an innovative compliment. But I realized she was talking about literary genre, because she had invited me to dinner with the intention of convincing me to write books for children.

I had spent the whole day walking around Rome immersed in a joy that was precisely childlike—I was like a kid gazing for the first time upon carousels, Ferris wheels, and improbable slides lowered from clouds. By eight or nine that night, though, an excellent Nebbiolo had lulled me toward sleep, and maybe that's why the editor felt she had to amp up her argument, which was by no means flattering: *Children's literature is a better fit for your style. As I see it, your novels are childish. Your books are picture books but they don't have illustrations, and we should fix that. I don't like your novels. Your children's books would be much, much better. Why write for adults when you should be writing for children?*

The next day she called me at the hotel because she'd woken up with the sense that she'd said too much. I told her she hadn't. "But I'm sure I said some stupid things," she insisted, in a voice that was sluggish from the hangover. "Your novels are extraordinary," she told me, and although I knew she was lying, I assured her that her words would give me the energy to keep going. She asked if I would actually be interested in writing for kids. I replied that I still didn't quite feel ready for my debut in children's literature.

It was an odd, funny situation. Now, as I think about those words, *childlike, childish, children's*, I remember that editor and consider the possibility that she was right, that she is right. During my college years, while I wrote my term papers driven by the sole desire to impress my professors, I started to sense the risk of forever losing the possibility of connecting with the people I really loved. From there, the rudiments of a style arose. More than addressing actual people, when I wrote I pictured a sort of nonexistent younger brother with whom I was eager to communicate. I wouldn't say that I have a style, because my idea of style has changed and will go on changing, but if I did have to play that game, the truth is that I would happily subscribe to something like a children's style, a childish style.

269

Your light body competes with the wind, prevails in the halted hammock.

270

The sky is full of warblers and red flycatchers. We find a gigantic papaya tree and a flamingo that curses tentative boats.

We celebrate your first words like sports reporters swollen with patriotic euphoria. We eat fried bananas, green pozole, and coconut ice cream.

On the way home you vomit all over the Oaxacan guayabera I was given for Father's Day in your name.

271

At night, the mourning geckos fornicate on the roof, lit by the fires of the bay.

Today you learned to imitate the bread seller's call.

279

A curator whom I have met a total of five times in my life but who considers me his close friend called at two in the morning to tell me he was thinking about having a child. "I want my life to change," the mezcal said through him.

Maybe he *is* my friend, I thought. And it's true that I do like him. I care about him. The first proof of my affection is that instead of telling him to go to hell, I reacted with caution. The second is that I've chosen to give him a different profession in case he ever reads this (he's not a curator, though maybe he should be: he'd be good at it).

Just as it is profoundly naive to have a child presuming that life will continue on unaltered, becoming a parent with the sole intention of inducing change is colossally stupid. I didn't put it like that to the curator, precisely because I care about him. But I did tell him. And he understood. Then I offered to let him do some field research: I invited him over for lunch so we could spend the whole afternoon with my son.

Men construct a particular idea of camaraderie that's based on memorable alcoholic binges that lead to an exhilarating blind alleyway of confessions and complicities. But we get to know each other more intensely when we spend an entire afternoon with a friend who is now a father and is delighted to have us over and who talks about all kinds of things, not necessarily fatherhood, but who no longer looks us in the eye, because his gaze is fixed on the kid, who at any moment could start walking and fall on his ass.

280

Just as I expected, the curator never showed up. He called several hours later to apologize. He said he'd had a lot of work to do and that I shouldn't worry, because he had gotten past his crisis: he was single now. I didn't know how to respond. "Congratulations," I finally said.

292

I change the lyrics and melodies of the best lullabies while I wash the dishes with a new technique.

302

"You can't bring liquids in," said a man at the Educal bookstore at the National Museum of Popular Cultures, in Coyoacán.

"What do you think is in this bottle-mamila-mamadera-biberón?" I replied, with you asleep in the sling. "Mezcal? Absinthe? Anisette? Pisco, rum, gin, sake, tequila, bacanora, aguardiente, vodka? Rubbing alcohol?"

That's not true, I only mentioned mezcal. I'm perfecting my answer now as I write. The thing about referring to the bottle with a variety of words from different countries is something I really do, out of nervousness. Faced with the possibility of making a mistake, I give all the options.

"It doesn't matter what's in it."

"It's water!"

"That's what I mean, water is a liquid."

"What if it were breast milk?"

"As I understand it, breast milk is also a liquid."

It was hard not to snipe. *As I understand it, breast milk is also a liquid.* I would like to make a movie just so that, in a very minor scene, a character could sport a T-shirt with that motto.

I was mad, but I also thought the situation was funny. And you were soundly and warmly asleep. I asked to speak with the manager, like they do in movies. And, like in movies, the manager appeared immediately. He confirmed the bookstore's policies. He said we couldn't come in with containers of liquids, "no matter their nature." I asked him if he meant the nature of the containers or of the liquids. He didn't answer.

I asked if that meant that this bookstore, which belonged to the state of Mexico, forbade the entrance of ten-month-old children. He told me that ten-month-olds and children of all ages were welcome in this and all bookstores of the United States of Mexico, and that was precisely why there was a section of books for infants (he used that word, *infants*).

I asked whether the bookstore had water dispensers or anything of the sort. He said no. I told him that in my country, it was normal to drink tap water, but in Mexico everyone advised against it. He made no comment.

I asked if he drank tap water. I asked if he had kids. He replied that those questions were too personal.

The employee looked at his boss as though drawing happy conclusions.

Then, in a fit of inspiration, it occurred to me to treat this big cheese the way people treat leading men in movies when they act like jerks: in one swift, glorious movement, I opened your bottle and dumped the liquid right onto that character's gleaming bald spot—no, son, of course I didn't do that. Not that I didn't long to, but my urgent thirst for revenge mattered much less to me than your thirst for water.

321

"What's past is prologue." I don't know if I agree with that character in *The Tempest*. Well, I guess I do. I rewrite that prologue, then, to the infectious beat of the rocking chair.

352

You wake up on my chest and try to smooth my hair with both hands.

364

A son and his father share the lounge chair and invent some less serious clouds.

365

You cried for four seconds and got lost right away, with
   beautiful solemnity, in your mother's eyes.
You were a ship at sea, and you recognized the approaching
   shore as a return.
I know people don't remember their own first birthdays. But
   we will remember yours.
To look at you now is to realize, in astonished humility, that
   there was a time when we didn't know how to walk,
   when we didn't know how to talk.

To look at you now is to accept, somberly, that there was a
    long time when you didn't exist.

Your existence changes the place of the sacred. Your arrival
    forever changes the word *courage*, and the meanings of all
    the words.

Jennifer Zambra

I f I had been a girl, my parents would have named me Jennifer Zambra. It was decided. That was practically the first thing I told your mother, flirting in a Prospect Heights diner. Actually, we started out talking about trees and migraines. And we mourned the death of Oliver Sacks as if he were a family member or a mutual friend.

Like shy ambassadors from exotic countries, or like team captains in the center of the pitch, we exchanged books by Emmanuel Bove and Tamara Kamenszain. For the first few minutes we were fighting our nerves, so we pored over the menus passionately; we must have looked like we were searching for typos. And then we talked shit about other people's confused love affairs, which were perhaps our own.

Until at last we looked straight into each other's eyes without too much precaution. It was a noisy whole minute of old-fashioned heterosexual silence. Then the sudden confessions rolled in, and the satisfying lists of likes and dislikes. And those ambiguous phrases that sound so much like promises.

I don't know where I got the idea to ask your mother what she would have been called if she'd been born a boy. There was some context, but I don't remember what it was. It was a bad move, now that I think about it, maybe the worst. Luckily, your mom didn't think it was such a weird question. I remember she unnecessarily smoothed her hair behind her ears, seeming to draw on a smile with the movement.

"You first," she said wisely.

So I suddenly found myself talking about Jennifer Zambra. There'd been a time during my childhood when I had fueled my resentment with thoughts of that name, inspired by who knows what famous actress, and which back then had seemed so foreign. My parents hadn't given a thought to the fact that the name would have doomed me to endless ridicule.

But eventually I grew fond of the scene of my parents in a Villa Portales apartment, quickly seduced by the splendid tinkling of that fantastical name. Maybe my sister, who was two years old then, had even managed to utter the name of her hypothetical successor.

Last names are prose, first names are poetry. There are people who spend their whole lives reading the inescapable novel of their own surname. But first names contain latent whims, intentions, prejudices, possibilities, emotions. And they're nearly always the only text that the mother and father write together.

And so, for their potential male child, my parents wrote a conventional poem, one that would neither shine nor grow dull in any anthology, while for their possible daughter they wrote a more daring one, groundbreaking and polemical. A name that toyed with boundaries.

In my adolescent years I used to think about Jennifer Zambra's difficult or solitary or scandalous life. I even dreamed about her. I'd see her bouncing a ball off a wall on the playground of an empty school. Or bored to tears at Midnight Mass. Or hiding away from the world to triumphantly braid her stunning raven hair in solitude.

I spent hours deciding which of my buddies Jennifer Zambra would sleep with and which she would rather be just friends with. I even tried to fall doubly in love—in fantasy and nonfiction—with one of my classmates. And maybe I succeeded.

But I would also often forget about her. Or I'd pretend to forget. Or I'd straight up deny her existence. And there were even times when I made fun of Jennifer Zambra. In front of everyone. I laughed at her name, the way she dressed, the way she did her makeup. I read entries from her diary out loud just to make a fool of her. Even though I was the one who wrote that diary.

What nonsense. It's not easy to make the people inside us talk. But it can be done. We punish fiction, we punish jokes, we punish dreams, music, we punish the characters who have lived with us for our entire lives. And in the end we realize that we are not mystery movies, we *are* mystery.

I talked to your mom about all of this that day in the diner. I should have felt the precise panic of talking too much a lot sooner than I did. Luckily, the waiter interrupted, apparently wanting to know if we were all right. Then your mother went to the bathroom and looked at her phone and the world interrupted, too, with some piece of urgent news that I don't remember but that slightly altered the script.

"Your turn," I told her, thinking she had forgotten my question.

"I know," she replied.

That was when your mother said your name, the name that is now yours alone, but that would have been hers if she had been XY.

"My parents were so convinced I would be a boy they didn't even come up with a short list of girls' names," said your mom, as though parodying the pose of a romantic heroine. "They had to improvise with me, they had to come up with a name on the fly."

While your mother dug into her cinnamon toast, I focused on that name that is now yours alone: on its resonance, its beauty. I love to think that you were already circling us on that nearly blind date. I'm positive you were out there somewhere, crouched and ready. Applying for life from the very first flirtation. Delighted to fill out the form.

"You could give your son that name," I said to your mom after a pause that may have been very long or quite short. "And I could give it to mine."

That second sentence was too much, and maybe the first one was, too. Because, come on, there are rules. Your mother looked at me as though begging me to stop talking. And it wasn't easy, I uttered even more sentences after those, but finally I managed to shut up.

"We can walk to the subway from here," she said then.

It wasn't a question or an invitation, but a thought said aloud. We waited for the check, paid it—in sum, all those actions took place, but I don't remember anything except the bitter sense that I had ruined a splendid time.

"You're really intense," she told me when we were almost at the subway stop.

It didn't seem like a positive review: two stars out of five, three at the most. I didn't know how to reply. I've always had this chronic problem of enthusiasm. That's what I should have said to her. But she smiled and took me by the arm for a few seconds, almost leaning against me.

"I'd like to be Jennifer Zambra's friend," she told me before we said goodbye. "I have a feeling we're going to be good friends. More than friends."

We hugged, she went down into the subway, laughing hard, and I stood for a long time watching the crowd. It had just gotten dark, the heat was waning, it was a perfect night to walk for hours. The story continues, of course, and it gets better and better. I'll tell you all about it later.

Trip and Crawl

(Teonanácatl Blues)

Teonanácatl. That's what the Mexica tribe used to call the mushroom known today as *pajarito*, or *little bird*. My friend Emilio recommended it as a treatment for my cluster headaches, and he was also the one who got me a generous dose in chocolate form. I stashed the squares in the fridge and awaited the first symptoms with resignation, though I sometimes entertained the naive fantasy that the drug's mere presence would keep the headaches at bay. Sadly, soon enough I felt one coming on, and it was the very day we had set aside for a first-aid course. I'd better explain that: after attending a clumsy and tedious introduction to first aid, Jazmina and I had invited other first-time parents, and even reserved the spacious house next door, to have a doctor give an alternative four-hour course. But in the early morning of the designated day, I woke up with that intense pain in the trigeminal nerve that for me is the unequivocal sign of an impending headache. My wife suggested that I forget about the course, stay home, and take *pajarito*.

At four in the afternoon, Jazmina left with our son, Silvestre, and I devoured the first square, ready for a brief, utilitarian trip. The chocolate was delicious, and now I think that that must have influenced my decision, after an impatient twenty-minute wait, to eat a second square. This time the effect was almost instantaneous: I felt like hands were reaching directly into my head to turn off the pain, like someone rearranging cables or deftly pressing the combination on a safe. It was a delightful, glorious sensation.

I don't want to go into too much detail about the misery this illness has caused me over the course of more than twenty years. Suffice to say that my headaches come roughly every eighteen months, and their corrosive company lasts between 90 and 120 days, during which the idea of cutting off my head starts to seem reasonable and prudent. Occasionally some medication or other has allowed me to mitigate the pain, but none had ever brought the miraculous results I was feeling from this little bird. *Teonanácatl*—I should have mentioned before that the word means *flesh of the gods*—had radically cleansed me. Of course, there was still the risk that the pain could return, but somehow I knew it wouldn't, that I would be safe for a long time (eleven weeks now and counting).

Maybe it was the joy of sudden health that reminded me of some Silvio Rodríguez lyrics that I hadn't heard in years: "La canción es la amiga / que me arropa y después me desabriga" ("A song is the friend / who clothes and then disrobes me"). I belted it at the top of my lungs. I only remembered the beginning of the song but I freely made up the rest, as if I had to persuade a whole arena that I knew the lyrics. More or less around then, maybe in parallel with my musical interlude, I got it into my head that my friend Emilio was actually my son. I was convinced, but at the same time the idea's formulation was hard to accept. Still, in retrospect it was a pretty reasonable association: Emilio doesn't suffer from cluster headaches himself, but he grew up watching his father, the children's author Francisco Hinojosa, struggle with them for decades. If I couldn't find a way to get over them, my son would eventually get used to my migrainous periods, just as Emilio had his father's. I felt a light sadness, like from bossa nova. I thought about how generous Emilio was, just as Silvestre would be in a few years. I imagined my son at twenty years old, telling a friend about his dad's awful headaches. I pictured Emilio, or rather I focused my imagination on his face, specifically on his bushy beard: at first slowly, realistically, meticulously, using an electric shaver, and then with a lot of foam and a stupendous straight razor, I shaved him. I even dabbed on some aftershave. I wanted to text him. I wrote:

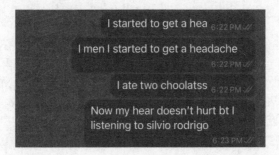

I started to get a hea   6:22 PM

I men I started to get a headache
                                    6:22 PM

I ate two choolatss   6:22 PM

Now my hear doesn't hurt bt I
listening to silvio rodrigo
                                    6:23 PM

Strictly speaking I hadn't listened to Silvio Rodríguez, but rather to my own voice singing his song, but that's how the thought took shape as I was writing the message.

Then the doorbell rang several times. I know there are people who think that ringing the doorbell over and over is an agreeable habit, but I am not one of them. When I leaned out the window, my annoyance turned to consternation, because it was Yuri. The singer, I mean. The person who had just rung the doorbell in that idiotic way was the famous Mexican singer Yuri, who, when she saw me leaning out the second-floor window, yelled: "I don't have cash for the taxi and this prick's waiting!" Teetering on heels that could easily pass for stilts, Yuri struck me as forceful, brave, and admirable. She shouted her imperious demand for money again; I had a five-hundred-peso bill, too much for a taxi, but I tossed it out the window to her anyway. She nimbly scooped it up and the driver handed her change; Yuri stashed it cheerfully in her bag and left without a goodbye.

I don't remember thinking that Yuri's presence might be a hallucination. I don't remember doubting her identity. Why was I so sure—and still am—that that little moocher was the singer Yuri? I did have the thought, as I made my way toward the bedroom (our apartment is very small, but my sense of space had shifted), that Yuri's husband was Chilean and an evangelical Christian, and that perhaps to Mexican eyes he and I looked alike. I definitely look Chilean, but maybe I also look evangelical—I look like an evangelical Chilean, I thought. That's when I became aware that I was high. A certain feeling of shock soon gave way to a giggle that sounded a bit false, diplomatic: maybe I was laughing just to prove I was capable of articulating laughter. And, like someone coming out of a long meeting in an unfamiliar city and calculating that he has a few hours free to have coffee and look around, I wanted to make the most of my trip, or rather I felt obligated to want to make the most of it. But since the purpose of my drug taking had been sadly therapeutic, I was unprepared for enjoyment. In a fit of pretentiousness, I considered writing something in a lysergic key. I also tried to read—there were several books on my bedside table—but it wasn't easy with my eyes so fuzzy. I fumbled around, earnestly and unsuccessfully, for my glasses. I texted Emilio again, looking for advice or maybe just attention:

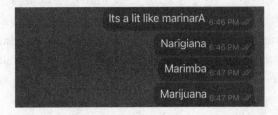

> Its a lit like marinarA   6:46 PM
> Narigiana   6:46 PM
> Marimba   6:47 PM
> Marijuana   6:47 PM

I meant that the effect was similar to that of marijuana, though I'm not sure that's what I really felt—it was more just a conversation starter. Emilio called me, and when he heard the high version of my voice he laughed, but also got very worried. He told me that half a chocolate square would have been enough to extinguish the pain. I told him I had shaved him, but he didn't understand, or maybe he thought I was just speaking Chilean. He asked where Jazmina and our son were. I told him they'd gone to a first-aid class, and he was incredulous—he inferred that my wife, on seeing me in this condition, had decided to go right out and take a class. It sounded like an illogical or extraordinarily slow reaction: something like dealing with an earthquake by reading a study on earthquakes. I explained the situation, and he was reassured. I said I was hungry and was going to order something from Uber Eats. He told me to call him if I needed anything at all.

Sensing the impending munchies, I ordered heaps of food. My purchase included tacos al pastor; brisket, chorizo, and pork tacos; volcanes de bistec; a fig tart; and three extra-large cups of horchata. I amused myself by watching the Uber map on my phone; Rigoberto's tiny bike was moving unusually fast. I suppose I expected it to move very slowly and the movement seemed less than slow and I translated that as speed. And from one moment to the next, that speed became alarming. Rigoberto is going to kill himself, I thought, and I pictured hundreds of cyclists, all wearing backpacks adorned with the Uber Eats or Rappi or Cornershop logo, stoically crisscrossing Mexico City, and I felt a hazy shiver.

The doorbell rang—a brief, prudent little chime—but I didn't think I'd be up to walking down the stairs. I sat on the top step and devised the brilliant plan of sliding down on my butt. After maybe half an hour I reached the bottom, and then I clung scrupulously to the wall like a Spider-Man in training. By the time I managed to get to the building's front door, Rigoberto was long gone. Later I realized he had called me and my phone was in my pocket, but I neither heard it ring nor felt it buzz. I went up the stairs in the same inelegant but safe manner I'd come down. The fog was spreading in my eyes; I felt I was in the middle of a dense cloud. I wanted to look for my glasses again, but was simply incapable. Then I discovered I was wearing them. I had been wearing my glasses the whole time. When I took them off I found that I could see fine, or as well as my astigmatism and myopia usually allowed me to see. I crawled to the kitchen and devoured everything I could find: some stiffened slices of cheddar cheese, a bunch of rice crackers, several anxious handfuls of uncooked oatmeal, three Chiapas bananas and two Dominico ones, and a few dozen arduous but delicious pistachios.

When I made it back to the bedroom, pretty desperate by now, I thought of *Octodad*, that agonizing and Kafkaesque video game where an octopus tries to wrangle his tentacles to carry out human activities. I've only played it once, but I've never forgotten how hard it was for Octodad to, say, pour a cup of coffee or mow the lawn or buy groceries. I lay on the floor like a ball of yarn and thought about Silvestre, and I wished someone would take me by the hands and walk me to where he was. I thought about my son learning to crawl.

"There are children who never crawl": that sentence arose in my head, spoken in the voice of a friend. "Some kids just go straight to walking." Specialists emphasize the importance of crawling for neurological development, but there are also people who claim that those specialists exaggerate. I remembered the story of a university professor with impeccable credentials who had a student over to her house and crawled during the entire visit. I mean: she crawled to open the door, accompanied her guest to the living room crawling, crawled to get a glass of water for her, and only after some small talk—made on all fours—did the professor explain to the flabbergasted student, with utter solemnity, that she had decided to spend three days crawling, because she hadn't crawled as a baby and wanted to rectify that disadvantage once and for all. Jazmina and I had laughed our heads off over that story, which now struck me as very sad or serious or enigmatic.

So without further ado, I decided to try crawling. I managed to plant my hands securely but not my knees, and then nailed my knees but not my hands. This happened several times. I turned over repeatedly on the floor, the way I'd rolled down sand dunes at the beach as a child. I lay on my back and managed to drag myself over the floor with my heels in a kind of inverse crawl. I lay on my belly again and tried using my toes and elbows, but I couldn't move forward: a slug would have beat me in a hundred-millimeter sprint. Then I concluded that I had never crawled. I'd asked my mother about this recently on the phone. "I'm sure you did. All babies crawl," she said. It bugged me that she didn't remember. She recalled that I learned to talk very early (she said this as though referring to an incurable disease) and that I started walking before I turned one, but she had no memory of me crawling. "All babies crawl," she told me, but no, Mom: not all of them do. Crawling is, in and of itself, fascinating, but so is not crawling—to get up suddenly, *à la* Lazarus, and simply walk, with spontaneous fluidity, without any visible learning process. To walk without having crawled is an admirable triumph of theory over practice. Then I went off on a tangent and found myself rigorously analyzing the song "La cucaracha," which seemed to reveal something about myself or Silvestre or about parenthood or life in general, something impossible to explain yet true, definite, and even measurable. I pictured Silvestre at eighty years old. I thought, with undeniable sadness, I will not be at my own son's eightieth birthday party, because by then I'll be . . . But I was incapable of adding eighty plus forty-three. I thought about the ending of *The Catcher in the Rye*. I thought about a story by Juan Emar. I thought about these beautiful lines by Gabriela Mistral: "The dancer is dancing now / the dance of losing all she had."

I leapt from one image to another as fast as someone reading only the first sentences of paragraphs. I wanted to sleep, I tried hard to summon sleep, but both my feet were planted firmly in the waking world. Then came an awful moment when I heard voices crying out for me—I knew I had to run over to the house next door, that they needed me there, but I couldn't do it and I felt utterly useless, I *was* utterly useless. I saw myself as a building whose windows were all smashed. I saw myself as a deflated yoga ball. I saw myself as a giant snail drooling slime on the floor where everyone would slip and slide. I again heard or imagined people calling for me, and I thought I could make out my wife's voice and my son's crying, and with a practically heroic reserve of energy, I managed to stand up and take a couple of steps before falling on my ass.

I lay aching on the floor and closed my eyes for several minutes. I wasn't sleepy, but I knew I still had the capacity to sleep. And I slept. The next thing I remember is that I felt better. Or rather, I thought I felt better, but I also mistrusted my feelings, so I started taking stock, awakening my senses. I ventured a careful, timid crawl. My knees ached a lot, which, maybe because of my Catholic upbringing, I interpreted as a positive sign. I reached the living room and stayed on all fours staring at the plants. Some beautiful ants, the blackest and shiniest and danciest ants in all of human history, were coming and going along a little path that began at a groove in the window and ended at the summit of a flowerpot. I looked at them intently: I absorbed them, I enjoyed them. I said something to them—more than one thing, I don't remember what. I concentrated on the plants. I called them by their names: Succulent, Bromeliad, Oleander.

I wrote this message to Jazmina; I felt better:

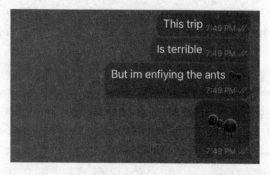

At a certain point I discovered it was dark out and that I could move with some degree of normalcy. The first-aid class must have been about to end, or maybe it was already over. I considered the possibility of doing nothing, a possibility I almost never consider. Instead, I decided to take some little excursions between the bedroom and the living room, practicing for my expedition to the house next door. There were a lot of excursions, judging by the time of the next message, which I sent to Jazmina immediately before going outside:

When I was finally sure I wouldn't take a nosedive, I welcomed the fresh nighttime air on my face like a blessing. I idealized the imminent scene, eagerly anticipating or more like foreseeing Jazmina and Silvestre, and in my imagination they coincided, they were once again a single person. But the first thing I saw when I opened the door was disconcerting: a bunch of grown-ups crawling around on the ground. For a fraction of a second I thought I was still midtrip, or that they had all taken *pajarito*, too, or that it wasn't a class on first aid but rather on crawling. One of the crawlers, perhaps the most diligent one, was Jazmina. When she saw me she got up, hugged me, and explained that the class was over but they'd been looking for the doctor's cell phone for the past hour. My breathing—or my sense of humor, more or less the same thing—returned to normal. Silvestre was asleep. I kissed his forehead and wanted to pick him up, but I desisted, just in case. Instead I joined the group of crawlers with ambition and bravura (Now *this* I can do well, I thought), moved by a competitive desire to vindicate myself by being the one to find the doctor's phone. Under the table I ran into my friend Frank, who looked bored or maybe rueful. He told me, in English so no one would understand (though I think everyone there understood English), that the doctor was overdoing it a little.

The doctor did, in fact, seem disproportionately dejected: she was crawling around like a baby searching for her most treasured rattle. Then she stood up and leaned against a window in a melancholic pose. She looked up at the ceiling and shook her head like someone trying, for the umpteenth time, to remember a name or an address or a prayer. The scene seemed to drag out forever, unbearably: fifteen or twenty minutes of the doctor mourning her lost cell phone.

I had been advised to drink cold milk to cut a trip short, but at that moment I thought the doctor needed it more than I did. She accepted the glass I handed her with apparent bafflement. Then came the sudden denouement, which was obvious, categorical, slipshod: Frank had accidentally put the damn phone at the bottom of a diaper bag. My friend gave the doctor a mischievous, contrite smile, but she wasn't having it: she drank her glass of milk solemnly and professionally, and left. We all left.

I picked up Silvestre and started humming a very fast version of Yuri's song "La maldita primavera." Jazmina laughed and yawned. We walked home with sure steps, with all the eagerness and joy of people returning after a long stay in another country. My son was sleeping soundly as I told him, with my eyes, not to ever crawl, not to ever walk, that it wasn't necessary: I could carry him in my arms his whole life.

Good Morning, Night

I

It's nighttime but I'm awake
you say in a newsworthy voice
so I turn on the radio
and for a few minutes we watch
the fleeting freezing sidewalks
and the vanishing point of phone lines
hung between utility poles

good morning, night, you say
and I burst into a laugh
that is also a yawn
I accept the new day
and change your diaper
with anonymous prowess

while I make breakfast
you seem absorbed in an invisible puzzle
but when I come back with the oatmeal

and half a mango
in the shape of a shell
I find you asleep
with your mouth hanging open
curled up on the sofa
placid as a cat on a rooftop

I sit down beside you
And drink a pot of coffee
Waiting for the dawn.

II

And he walked and he walked
until one day he reached
the kitchen

and he walked and he walked
until one day he reached
the bathroom

and he walked and he walked
until one day he reached
the bed

and he fell asleep
and   if   you   looked   at   his   eyelids

vibrating full dream ahead

he seemed to still be walking
and he jumped higher than high
and grew bigger than big.

III

The day of your second birthday
you didn't want to hit your own piñata
thanks Daddy, but you hit it, you told me

and you moved your right hand
to the contagious beat of the *dale dale dale*
                              no pierdas el tino
                              porque si lo pierdes
                              pierdes el camino

I'm ringing a bell, you told me
I can't hit the piñata
because   my   hand   is   busy
ringing a bell

I told you that you could hit the piñata
using your right hand
and go on ringing
that imaginary bell
with your left
and you looked at me as if to say no, Dad,
that's impossible
it makes no sense.

French for Beginners

You want the book about the mole, which you've been reading with your mother all the time lately, but it's in French, a language I speak badly—"You do know French, Dad," you say, to encourage me. I was expecting you to complain, even cry, but instead you talk to me as if you were the father and I a boy with stage fright.

I search your shelves for that elusive little rectangular book with the hope of not finding it, but I see it right away. I consider pretending I can't find it, but I don't want to lie to you—I don't want to lie, and at the same time I want you to believe, to go on believing, that I know French. Or maybe what I want is for my mere desire to read you this book to cause a solid prior knowledge of the French language to miraculously appear inside my head. Because I want to read it to you well, without omissions or hesitations. I want there to be music. The first thing we do every morning is listen to music and dance. And when we flop onto the sofa to read, I want literature to be a natural continuation of that music—I want it to be another kind of music.

The mole book is a great story, and it also harmonizes with your recent zeal for all things scatological: someone has pooped on the mole's head, and instead of cleaning it he decides to use it as evidence to find the culprit, so off he goes to talk to the pigeon, sporting the turd like a topknot or a crown. The pigeon claims innocence and straightaway produces a spontaneous evacuation that looks nothing at all like the turd the protagonist is wearing on his head. The poor mole is brave and dignified as he confronts his other suspects, but the hare, the goat, the cow, and the hog all produce their own fecal samples that serve as irrefutable alibis, so he has no choice but to consult the expert opinion of some flies who land on his poop crown and conclude beyond a shadow of a doubt . . .

You already know how it ends. Endings, for you, are not tied to closure, they don't represent the finish line but rather an intermediate position, like when a cyclist completes a lap but still has several rounds to go before the race is over. And really, that's how literature for adults functions too, though we tend to ignore that fact; we tend to surrender to the superstition of the ending, the denouement, because sometimes we need to assume that stories end, obediently, on the final page.

I do my best to translate, improvising different and hopefully funny voices for the animals in the story. There are moments when I feel like I'm getting away with it, but no, it's not going well, and you know it. I can tell you're not focusing, as you usually do, only on the pictures: you're also looking at those obscure words that you associate with the characters' familiar phrases. Though you know that reading with me is not the same as reading with your mother, you're put off by how different my version is from hers. You correct me, perfect my translation as we go. In the rereading, the first rereading, I incorporate those nuances that I missed the first time and that you've just explained, so the story flows better and my performance can evolve—the mole's voice, for example, can be funnier.

You know the mole's story to perfection. By this point you could almost read it yourself, although for now reading is something you do through your mother or me or your grandmother or any other adult who's nearby. There are days when you say "Read to me," but you also often say "I want to read," which of course doesn't mean you want to learn how to read for yourself, but that you want me to read for you, or maybe more precisely that you want what happens when we read to happen, because what happens is different every time, we know that by now: between reading and rereading, in a matter of seconds, the book has changed and we have changed, too; we pause at different moments, we play a game made up of interruptions and continuations that is always new.

Back when you were just starting to walk, you would see me reading and you'd climb up on my lap to get between the book and my eyes, the way cats do, though you had the courtesy not to scratch the pages. You soon lost that deference, though, and your curiosity turned to rebellion: seeing me read alone, in silence, became intolerable for you, and you would snatch the book away or tear the page. And it's true that silent reading does seem individualistic, stingy, shabby. These days when you catch me in the miserly act of reading to myself, you ask me to read out loud and I always do, so you've already heard a few sentences by Jenny Offill and a

48 *Childish Literature*

couple of lines by Idea Vilariño, and even two or three paragraphs of *The Magic Mountain*.

No one taught you anything about music—there was no need. Music was just there, from before you were born; no one had to explain what it was, what it is, how it works. No one has explained literature to you either, and hopefully no one ever will. Silent reading is a sort of conquest; those of us who read in silence and solitude learn, precisely, how to be alone, or maybe it's more like we capture a less aggressive solitude, a solitude emptied of anxiety; we feel inhabited, multiplied, accompanied, as we read in our sonorous silent solitude. But you will learn all this for yourself in a few years, I know. You will decide for yourself whether you're still interested in the form of knowledge that literature enables, so strange, so specific, so hard to describe.

We read in the morning and sometimes also in the afternoon, and every night your mother or I read you three stories at bedtime. You won't accept one story or two, it has to be three. And you never ask us to repeat any of the three bedtime stories. It's now, in the morning, when you seem to prefer the repetition of the same story. Maybe diurnal books function for you more like music and the nocturnal ones are properly stories, but I don't want to jump to conclusions, because on the other hand they're the same books, it's not that there are separate repertoires of daytime and nighttime stories (the only stable and enigmatic category is the one you call "poop books," which, oddly, does not include the mole story). It also sometimes happens that in the morning you ask me for the story we read the night before, as if during the eight or nine hours you slept the book had been hanging there, hovering above you in your bed.

Every night, storytime builds an imminence or a threshold: it's the stretch of the journey we can only traverse by sailing. When we read, flashlight in hand, *The Game of Shadows* by Hervé Tullet, the ceremony lengthens out interminably, and a similar thing happens with *The Book with No Pictures* by B. J. Novak, which makes you cackle ferociously, or with *The Smelly Book* by Babette Cole, or with almost any of the magnificent stories by Gianni Rodari. Really there are a lot of books that work against us, because instead of building to the brink of sleep, they wake you up a little more: suddenly you seem convinced that sleeping is a waste of time. But what the hell, literature's function has never been to induce anyone to sleep. Sometimes reading riles up your imagination, which is always pretty riled up anyway, but even so it helps to end the day on a high note. What matters is the ritual, of course, the ceremony. The company.

In his beautiful book *Reads Like a Novel*, Daniel Pennac laments that he and his wife stopped reading stories to their son when he learned to read for himself. But maybe it wasn't the mother's or father's fault. Maybe it was the boy himself who decided to leave them out of the reading ceremony. Your mom and I don't want that to happen. Reading doesn't fall under the category of things that we do for you until you learn to do them alone. It's not like brushing your teeth or trimming your nails.

Nor is it like walking, although I tend to think it's similar. We carried you in our arms until you learned to walk, and we still carry you when you're tired and sometimes you're not tired and we carry you anyway, and we will go on doing it as long as we can bear your weight and you can bear the symbolic weight of having us carry you. Now you read through us, but once you can read for yourself it might stop seeming fun to have us read to you. We'll have to come up with something, some way to continue the ritual, which is the most important one of the day; may it change shape, but may it go on happening.

After the stories comes the music, the last music of the day. Always, since your very first days of life, I sing "Beautiful Boy," but the other songs are not lullabies. Maybe "Two of Us" has something of the lullaby about it, though it's not a song about fathers and sons but rather love and companionship, and that's why I sing it to you. The rest of the songs—by Violeta Parra, Silvio Rodríguez, Andrés Calamaro, Los Jaivas—are love songs or protest songs or songs of love and protest.

Your mother and I take turns every night with the ritual of the three books and the three or four (or five) songs. Mornings, however, always start with me. I, who used to be a night owl, now get up early with you: we have watched the sunrise together almost every day of your life. You haven't always appreciated that I was your unconditional morning companion, though. In times that now seem remote, you would give me a look that was a mixture of suspicion and something serious or haughty that I don't know how to define. You would cry for twenty seconds, sometimes a full minute, before accepting my consolation. I guess the living room was like the bar where you came to cry out your breastfed heartaches, and I was the bartender who knew just how you liked your orange juice, or the bland but friendly regular who was always willing to listen and laugh at your jokes and pay your tab.

"Let's keep going, Dad," you say to me now, on this particular morning. I don't feel like reading the mole story for a third time, but I know that in this case *keep going* means *keep reading the same book*. In the middle of this third reading, your mother appears in the living room and attentively salutes the sun while we read the mole story for a fourth, a fifth time, and judging by her sly smile I figure I am barely scraping by in the French literature lesson. "Thank you," you say to me, in any case, before leaving with your grandmother, who has just come by to take you to Chapultepec Park. I'm pleased and proud whenever you remember to give thanks, but this time it also throws me off and moves me, because it's the first time you have thanked me for the reading or the company or whatever it is you're thanking me for—I'm really not clear on it. *Thank you for having read that book in French even though you don't know French. Thank you for trying to overcome your intellectual limitations to entertain me.* Maybe you mean something like that.

I should head to the service room on the roof where I usually work, but before going up I make more coffee and return to the sofa to read the story of the mole again, I don't know why. Well, there's no mystery there: it's because I miss you. It happens to me a lot, and to your mom, too: just when we finally have time to work, we're distracted by your absence.

I turn the pages, in training to read you this story again in the near future. Though it doesn't have many words, this is, strictly speaking, the first book I have read in French. It's a funny realization, because French is the language of Marguerite Duras, Flaubert, Perec, and Bove, among other authors I have tried to read in the original. In those cases, though the results may sometimes be decent, they're always false or fraudulent, since I've already read those authors' books in Spanish translations, and there are passages that I know by heart and unfamiliar words I figure out from context or don't mind not knowing.

Yes, the story of the mole is the first book I have truly read in French, and the fact that you were the one who helped me read it strikes me as a crucial, beautiful, telling detail. Only now do I notice the story's title, because with children's books—this is obvious, but I have only just discovered it—titles fulfill a different function, they matter less. The truth is I don't know the titles of many of the books we've read together; like you, I don't identify them by the title but by the animal or color on the cover or the size of the book, so it's not at all strange that I don't know the grandiose title of the mole story: *De la petite taupe qui voulait savoir qui lui avait fait sur la tête*, which in English would be something like *About the little mole that wanted to know who had done that on his head* (I see online that there's an English edition called *The Story of the Little Mole Who Went in Search of Whodunit*).

Titles aren't important in children's literature, and perhaps authors matter even less. That's what I think when I notice the perfectly German names of the author and illustrator of the mole book: Werner Holzwarth and Wolf Erlbruch. Only then do I comprehend that our book is a translation, as I confirm in the tiny print of the credits: *Vom kleinen Maulwurf, der wissen wollte, wer ihm auf den Kopf gemacht hat*. That's the original title.

I ask your mom why she bought the book in French and not Spanish. She says they were out of the Spanish edition, and that she would have bought it in German or Japanese or in any other language because she thinks it's great and she knows it by heart, her mom used to read it to her when she was little. When she reads it with you she barely glances at

the printed words, she just operates on memory; she's sure
that she is reading with the same words her mother read in the
Spanish book—the Spanish translation—that they had in
their house. I ask what happened to her old Spanish mole
book. She tells me that at some point her mom donated all
the books they used to read together to a library.

I go up to the rooftop office thinking about that earnest and
outraged mole who moves down through the generations with
a funny turd on his head. Your grandmother, your mother,
and you are suddenly one single person who speaks, listens,
and smiles. You also have storybooks at your grandmother's
house, books I don't always know about. "These chocolates
are going to get a coup d'état," you said one day, and I spent
hours thinking about where you had learned the expression
coup d'état, and even started to feel guilty for having let it slip
carelessly without explaining its horrendous meaning to you.
But then I went to your grandmother's house and saw the big
Mafalda collection and understood. I read you some jokes in
an Argentine accent, like I do with books by Liniers or Isol,
but you just stared at me, disconcerted and then furious, because your grandma "translates" them to Mexican. "Mafalda
isn't Argentine, Dad!" you yelled, on the verge of tears.

Suddenly I let my mood darken at the evidence, which my
parents confirmed, that no one ever read me stories at bedtime. It's a self-pitying thought, weak and easy. I recall my
grandmother, who instead of reading us stories would tell us
all kinds of gossip about the community she lost when she
was young, in the 1939 earthquake in Chillán. Almost all of
her childhood friends had died in that earthquake, but their
stories remained, and my grandmother savored them as she

called them up for my sister and me. Then, out of nowhere she would remember that the protagonists of her fictions were all dead, and she would feel their absence and start crying, and we had to climb into her bed and console her. Those stories were our Latin, as Natalia Ginzburg would say. Maybe when I started writing, years later, I wanted to honor and imitate the swings between laughter and tears that occurred when we listened to my grandmother.

I try to get back into the novel I'm working on, but this time I'm distracted by the thought, also somber, that books are not like clothes that we outgrow and give away. On the spot I decide, with ridiculous solemnity, that we will never get rid of the books we read with you, because it would be like throwing away photo albums; I think of those books, your books, as documents, and I want to store them away as if they were locks of your hair or the first ultrasound images. It's a silly thought, especially coming from me, because before moving to Mexico I gave away my entire library. I didn't think it made sense to change countries lugging dozens of boxes of books that I would perhaps never even read again.

Your room already held a small library when you arrived. As soon as we found out you were coming, your mom and I started spending hours in the children's sections of bookstores in search of your future books; even when we knew nothing about you, we already knew some of the books we would read together. Since then we always make sure there are new stories around so you don't get bored, but really, we're the ones at risk of boredom.

Your library is that other, lost, library of mine, shrunk to miniature and of course perfected, because it remains untouched by the *tsundoku* that spreads like a virus over the house's other shelves, so full of books-to-read that sometimes looking at them is like checking the stack of bills to be paid. Your crowded shelves hold no unopened, ignored books. We have read all of your books, by now, at least ten times.

I make some progress in my novel, though while I write I keep thinking about your books, about children's books, and about my own spectacular ignorance. After a cursory five-minute Google search, I learn that the mole story is an absolute classic of children's literature, and that not knowing it is like having no idea who Sandro Botticelli or Martina Navratilova are. Picture book, illustrated hardcover, comic book, cartoon, graphic novel . . . I go over the concepts like when I had to memorize the Köppen climate classification groups, or as if I were prepping to impart a master class. But I don't have to give a lecture. All I have to do is sit beside you, that's all, and read to you the parts of the book that have words, while you read all the rest. And it's perhaps more important to realize that it's the words that are *all the rest*.

It seems so absurd to me that there is such a thing as non-children's literature, literature for adults, for non-children, a literature-literature that is the real literature; the idea that I write and read a real literature and the books you and I read together are a kind of substitute or alternative or preparation for real literature seems as unfair as it is false. And honestly, I don't see any less literature in a story by Maurice Sendak or María Elena Walsh than in any of my favorites from "grown-up literature." It seems impossible, it's true, to imagine you reading my books: the ones I've written or the novel I'm trying to write now. The stories are almost always sad and perhaps unnecessary; before you read them I would have to explain so many things, things that you could probably understand but that I'm not sure I would be able to explain.

I head back down to the apartment with the excuse of eating a granola bar, and I go into your room. I look at your clothes, your bookshelves. We've already given away a lot of your clothes, and I love seeing, for example, a friend's little girl sporting your old solar system T-shirt. But it's hard for me to imagine someday giving away your books or your little red guitar or your astronaut suit.

You, of course, will be the one who decides whether or not to get rid of those books, which might be in the way when you want to step down, once and for all and forever, from childhood and childish things. I stand gazing at the chaotic shelf, and suddenly understand that those books whose titles I don't remember, written by people whose names I don't know, are exactly the kind of books that I want to write from now on.

Crowd

I dream about a guy I used to see years ago in New York, standing on a corner in Bryant Park or at the entrance to Grand Central Station, classifying people: *tourist, not a tourist, tourist, tourist, not a tourist,* he intoned, in a voice that was mechanical and at the same time oddly friendly. He was about six feet tall and had long, unkempt red hair and green eyes embedded in a face that reflected extreme, sustained concentration. The man was genuinely dedicated to his ambitious project of classifying all the faces in the crowd, and I got the impression that he was pretty accurate, though sometimes he hesitated or made mistakes. With me, for example: my immigrant's face almost always led him to consider me "not a tourist," but a few times he put me in the tourist camp.

In the dream, everything happens just like in my memories, only we're not in Bryant Park or at Grand Central but on some equally overcrowded corner in Mexico City or Santiago de Chile. I don't know if the crazy guy looks at me or classifies me, but his presence makes me happy, it feels like a good omen. On the next corner I run into a friend—someone I don't know and have never seen, but in the dream we're friends—who is doing the same thing as the crazy guy, though she doesn't seem crazy but rather overwhelmed or angry or

both. I want to stop and talk to her, but I know I can't interrupt her task. Now I'm sure I'm in Santiago and I'm walking
toward the mountains (which I don't see or look for, but I
know they're there). I speed up, wanting to know if someone
will also be on the next corner carrying out that absurd and
horrible job. They should have a spreadsheet, they're going to
forget, I think, and then I look at the crowd and another
thought emerges, vague and disruptive, something like, This
is a crowd, or, I'm in a crowd, and then the force of those
words mixes with my son's voice and I wake up.

It's five fifteen in the morning and my son has turned on his
Miffy lamp. I pick him up and tell him, as always, that night
is for sleeping and day for playing, and he looks at me with
compassion, the way you look at a person who insists on a
cause that is clearly futile. Until a few weeks ago, when Silvestre woke up before dawn, we would go to the window and
play a game of counting the red or white or blue cars—he
always got to pick the color—which at that hour were already starting to abound, or else we would guess the names
of the pedestrians running toward the metro with their urgent wet hair. Now there is no one on the sidewalk and cars
pass very rarely, and I sense that my son is going to ask me
again, as he does every day now, where all the people are,
and I even prepare my reply. But he doesn't ask; instead, he
falls asleep and sighs against my chest.

Aided by the indecisive rhythm of the rocking chair, I
think about my dream, about the crowd that has suddenly
turned abstract, undefined, extemporaneous. It's not unusual
for me to dream about crowds; on the contrary, my dreams
tend to be full of extras who turn into secondary characters,

and secondary characters who suddenly take on starring roles, but I wonder if this dream, this crowd, is new. Perhaps all the people in my dream also dreamed about teeming streets last night. I get caught up in the idea, that lyrical fancy. I think about the people who have spent the whole pandemic dreaming of impossible crowds. I think of my friends in Chile who were out protesting in the streets two months ago, and are now, individually revisiting collective dreams. I think about the arguable beauty of the word *multitude*, the word *crowd*. About what that word shows and what it hides.

I remember one evening on the subway, when I was twelve. There were a lot of us at that hour, around 8:00 p.m., returning from our schools in downtown Santiago to our houses in Maipú. The buses promised fun or at least company, but that night I decided to take the subway, which would get me home faster and without running into anyone. I was sad, I don't remember why. I do remember the moment when, a few seconds before getting out at the Las Rejas stop, I looked at the crowd that I was part of and thought something like, They all have lives, they're all going home, everyone is missing something or has too much of another thing, they are all sad or happy or tired. Years later, when I learned the concept of *epiphany*, I immediately knew what experience to associate with it.

After breakfast, we listen to music and then sit on the floor to draw with my son's crayons. It seems like he's entertaining himself on his own, so I pour another cup of coffee and take up a position at the window. The sun is gaining ground on the horizon, but the day doesn't seem to have started. I count a scant ten cars, a couple of motorcycles, and three masked men, who of course are not tourists but vulnerable, gruff, melancholic workers. More and more people are managing to stay home, and the evocation of the absent crowd somehow soothes me. Still, I miss the full, noisy street from just a few weeks ago.

Suddenly I realize I've been preoccupied for a long time, and I feel the guilt of having neglected my son and the immediate joy of seeing that he's still there, intent on his work, concentrated, autonomous. I look at his beautiful, chaotic drawing. A few days ago he decided that crayons were fruit, and he started using them to draw passionate scribbles that he calls *smoothies*. I sit down beside him, help him hold the paper.

"Is it a smoothie?" I ask him.

"No," he tells me, categorically.

"What is it?"

"It's you, Dad, looking out the window."

Screen Time

I.

Many times over his two years of life, the boy has heard laughter or cries coming from his parents' bedroom. And who knows how he would react if he ever found out what his parents were really doing while he slept: watching TV.

He has never watched TV or seen anyone watching it, so his parents' television is vaguely mysterious to him: its screen is sort of a mirror, but the reflection it gives is opaque, unsatisfactory, and you can't even draw in the steam like on the bathroom mirror, though sometimes a layer of dust allows for similar games.

Still, the boy wouldn't be surprised to learn that this screen reproduces moving images. He has occasionally been allowed to interact with images of people, most often people in his second country. Because the boy has two countries: his mother's, which is his primary one, and his father's, which is his secondary country, where his father doesn't live but his paternal grandparents do—they are the people the boy sees on-screen most often.

He has also seen his grandparents in person, because the boy has traveled twice to his second country. He remembers nothing of the first trip, but by the second he could walk and talk himself blue in the face, and those weeks were filled with new experiences, though the most memorable event happened on the flight there, a couple of hours before landing in his secondary country, when a screen that seemed every bit as useless as his parents' TV lit up and a friendly red monster emerged, talking about himself in the third person. The monster and the boy were fast friends right away, perhaps because back then the boy also talked about himself in the third person.

II.

To tell the truth the meeting was serendipitous, because the boy's parents hadn't planned to turn on the screen during that trip. The flight started out with a couple of naps, and then his parents opened the little suitcase that held seven books and five zoomorphic puppets, and much of the long flight was spent on the reading and immediate rereading of those books, accentuated by the puppets' interjections and the occasional comment on cloud shape or snack quality. Everything was going swimmingly until the boy asked for a stuffed animal that had chosen to travel—as his parents explained—in the hold of the plane, and then he remembered several others that—who knows why—had decided to stay behind in his primary country. Then, for the first time in six hours, the boy burst into tears that lasted a full forty seconds, which isn't a long time but, to a man in the row behind them, seemed very long indeed.

"Make that brat shut up!" bellowed the man.

The boy's mother turned around and looked at him with serene contempt. After a well-executed pause, she lowered her gaze to stare fixedly between his legs and said, without the slightest trace of aggression:

"Must be really tiny, huh?"

The man apparently had no defense against such an accusation, and didn't reply. The boy moved to his mother's arms, and now it was the father who knelt in his seat to stare back at the man. He didn't insult him, but merely asked his name.

"Enrique Lizalde," said the man, with the little dignity he had left.

"Thanks."

"Why do you want to know?"

"I have my reasons."

"Who are you?"

"I don't want to tell you, but you'll find out. Soon enough, you'll know full well who I am. Very soon."

The father glared several more seconds at the now remorseful Lizalde, and he would have kept right on provoking him except that a bout of turbulence forced him to refasten his seat belt.

"*I hope this motherfucker thinks I'm really powerful,*" the father murmured then, in English, which was the language the boy's parents instinctively used for insults or expletives when they were in his presence.

"*We should at least name a character after him,*" said the mother, also in English.

"*Good idea! I'll name all the bad guys in my books Enrique Lizalde.*"

"*Me too! I guess we'll have to start writing books with bad guys,*" she said.

And that was when they decided to turn on the screen in front of them and tune in to the show of the cheerful, furry red monster. They watched for twenty minutes, and when they turned off the screen the boy protested, but his dad explained that the monster's presence wasn't repeatable—he wasn't like books, which could be read over and over.

During the three weeks they spent in his secondary country the boy asked about the monster daily, and his parents explained that he only lived on airplanes. The reunion finally came on the flight home, and it lasted another scant twenty minutes. Two months later, since the boy kept talking about the monster with a certain melancholy, they bought him a stuffed replica, which in his eyes was the original. Since then the two have been inseparable: in fact, right now, the boy has just fallen asleep hugging the furry red toy, and his parents have already headed to the main bedroom: if things happen as they have been lately, this story is likely to end with the scene of the two of them in bed, watching TV.

III.

The boy's father grew up with the TV always on, and at his son's age he was possibly unaware that the television could even be turned off. His mother, on the other hand, had been kept away from TV for an astonishing length of time: ten whole years. Her parents' official version was that the TV signal didn't reach the corner of the city where they lived, so that to the mother the TV seemed, as it does now to her son, like a completely useless object. One day she invited a classmate over to play, and without asking anyone, the friend simply plugged in the TV and turned it on. There was no disillusionment or crisis: the girl thought the TV signal had only just reached their neighborhood. She ran to relay the good news to her mother, who, though she was an atheist, fell to her knees, raised her arms to the sky, and shouted histrionically, persuasively, "Holy mother of God! It's a miracle!"

In spite of these very different backgrounds, the woman who grew up with the TV permanently off and the man who grew up with it permanently on are in complete agreement that it's best to put off their son's exposure to TV as long as possible. In any case, they're not fanatics, they're not against TV by any means. It would be ironic if they were, because it had happened more than once, back when they were getting to know each other, that they turned to the time-honored strategy of meeting up to watch movies as a pretext for sex. Later, in the period that could be considered the boy's prehistory, they succumbed to the spell of many excellent series. And they never watched as much TV as during the months leading up to the birth of their son, whose intrauterine life was set not to Mozart symphonies or lullabies, but rather to the theme songs of series about bloody power struggles set in an imprecise ancient time of zombies and dragons or the spacious government house of the self-designated "leader of the free world."

When the boy was born, the couple's TV experience changed radically. At the end of the day, their physical and mental exhaustion allowed for only thirty or maybe forty minutes of waning concentration, so that almost without realizing it they lowered their standards and became habitual viewers of extremely mediocre series. They still wanted to venture into unfathomable realms and live vicariously through challenging and complex experiences that forced them to seriously rethink their place in the world, but that's what the books they read during the day were for; at night they wanted easy laughter, facile dialogue, and scripts that granted the sad satisfaction of understanding without making the slightest effort.

They would like, maybe a year or two down the road, to brighten a Saturday or Sunday afternoon by watching TV with the boy, and they even occasionally update a list of the movies they want to watch together as a family. But for now, the TV is relegated to that final hour of the day when the boy is asleep and the mother and father return, momentarily, to being simply she and he.

IV.

She is in bed looking at her phone and he is lying face up on the floor as if resting after a round of sit-ups. Suddenly he gets up and lies on the bed, too, and reaches for the remote but finds the nail clippers instead, so he starts to clip his fingernails. She looks at him and thinks that lately, he is always clipping his nails.

"We're going to be shut in for months. He's going to get bored," she says.

"They'll let people walk their dogs, but not their kids," he says bitterly.

"I'm sure he doesn't like this. He doesn't show it, he seems happy, but he must be having a horrible time. How much do you think he understands?"

"About as much as we do."

"And what do we understand?" She sounds like a student reviewing a lesson before a test.

"That we can't go out because there's a shitty virus. That's all."

"That what used to be allowed is now forbidden. And what used to be forbidden still is."

"He misses the park, the bookstore, museums. Same as we do."

"And the zoo," she says. "He misses the zebras especially, the giraffes, and that rabbit, the teporingo, that he likes so much. He doesn't say it, but he complains more, gets mad more. Not a lot, but more."

"He sure doesn't miss school, though," he says.

"I hope it's only for two or three months. What if it's more? A whole year?"

"I don't think so," he says. He'd like to sound more convinced.

"What if this is our world from now on? What if after this virus there's another and another?" She asks the question but it could just as well be him, with the same words and the same anxious intonation.

During the day they take turns: one of them watches their son while the other hides away to work. They need work time because they're behind on everything, and although everyone is behind on everything, they feel sure that they're a little more behind than everyone else. And yet they both offer to watch the boy full time, because that half day with him is a time of true happiness, genuine laughter, purifying escapism—they would rather spend the whole day playing ball in the hallway or drawing involuntarily monstrous creatures on the small square of wall they use as a blackboard or strumming guitar while the boy turns the pegs until it's out of tune or reading stories that they now find perfect, much better than the hopelessly "adult" books they write, or try to. Even if they only had one of those children's stories they would prefer to read it over and over, incessantly, rather than sit down in front of their computers with the awful news radio in the background to send email replies full of apologies for their lateness while glancing out of the corner of their eyes at the stupid map of real-time contagion and death— he looks, especially, at his son's secondary country, which of course is still his primary one, and he thinks of his parents and imagines that in the hours or days since he last talked to them they've gotten sick and he'll never see them again, and then he calls them and those calls leave him shattered, but he doesn't say anything, at least not to her, because she's spent weeks now in a slow and imperfect anguish that makes her think she should learn to embroider, or at least stop reading the beautiful and hopeless novels she reads, and she also thinks that she should have become something other than a writer, they agree on that, they've talked about it many times, because so often, every time they try to write, they feel the inescapable futility of each and every word.

"Let's let him watch movies," she says. "Why not? Only on Sundays."

"At least then we'd know if it's Monday or Thursday or Sunday," he says.

"What's today?"

"Tuesday. No, Wednesday."

"Let's decide tomorrow," she says.

He finishes cutting his nails and looks at his hands with uncertain satisfaction, or maybe like he's just finished cutting someone else's nails, or like he's looking at the nails of a person who just cut their own nails and was asking him, for some reason (maybe he's become an expert or an authority on the matter), for his opinion or approval.

"They're growing faster," he says.

"Didn't you just cut them last night?"

"That's what I'm saying, they're growing faster." He says this seriously, in a somber, scientific voice. "Every night I look at them and they've grown out during the day. Abnormally fast."

"Apparently it's good for nails to grow fast. I've heard that they grow faster at the beach." She speaks in the tone of a person who is trying to remember something, maybe the feeling of waking up on the beach with the sun in her face.

"I think mine are a record."

"Mine are growing faster too," she says, smiling. "Even faster than yours. By noon they're practically claws. And I cut them and they grow again."

"I think mine grow faster than yours."

"Prove it."

Then they put their hands together as if they could really see their fingernails growing, as if they could compare speeds, and what should be a quick scene lengthens out, because they let themselves get caught up in the absurd illusion of that silent competition, beautiful and useless, which lasts so long that even the most patient viewer would turn off the TV in indignation. But no one is watching them, though the TV screen is like a camera recording their bodies frozen in that strange and funny pose. A monitor amplifies the boy's breathing, and it's the only sound that accompanies the contest of their hands, their fingernails, a contest that lasts several minutes, but of course not long enough for anyone to win, and that ends, finally, with the burst of warm, frank laughter that they were really needing.

Childhood's Childhood

Daddy, let's play hide-and-seek with the virus," my son said, a little over a year ago now. I was surprised and saddened that he would talk about the virus with such familiarity, but it made sense. The pandemic had already started to transform his life—for better and for worse, because he missed the walks through Chapultepec Park just as intensely as he rejoiced over his canceled preschool (he wasn't a fan of his incipient academic life).

Hiding from the virus, in any case, was more reasonable than hiding from the ceiling or the refrigerator, as he would often suggest to me then, or from the Bible or Shakespeare's *Complete Works*, as I would suggest to him. So we huddled under the table and screamed fake screams of fear—fake because they were whispered imitations of screams, and also because the fear was fake, in theory, though at that moment I really was afraid. Or maybe it was fatalism that I felt—a fatalism that now, in retrospect, strikes me as a barely diminished version of optimism.

What will my son remember of this horrible year? I ask myself this question every day, and though I sometimes reply blithely, almost joyfully, that he will remember nothing, more often I get stuck in a sense of consternation, because it's strange and sad to imagine or somehow *know* that the same little human with his three years of life—and his twenty-nine pounds and forty inches—whom we have watched grow and whose life seems at times more real and always more valuable than our own, in a not so distant future will forget everything or almost everything he experienced in this past that we stubbornly insist on calling *present*.

Looked at from a perhaps overstated adulthood, it's easy to suppose that episodic memory starts at around three or four years old—in other words, before that age, we were simply incapable of remembering things. But anyone who has witnessed a child growing up knows that at three or even two years old, kids can remember what they did last week or last summer, and the memories are pure, not implanted, sometimes surprisingly precise and other times just as vague and fickle as everyone else's.

The big questions about the workings of human memory have their humble analogue in the emotion or disquiet we all feel when we think about those years that we erased, omitted, lost. What, really, was a full day like when we were ten months or two years old? Maybe later on, when we were teenagers, we heard a few authoritarian phrases ("I taught you to speak, I fed you, everything you have is thanks to me") and could thereby intuit or imagine those years of overwhelming dependence, but only once we become parents or occupy the space of parents and our backs hurt and we haven't slept well in weeks or months can we really conceive of that care we never thank them for simply because we don't remember it.

If we were like Funes, Borges's famous character who is unable to forget, we would go through life paralyzed by endless grudges and automatic, obligatory expressions of gratitude. That mysterious childish amnesia allows us to forget all the factors that could neutralize the severity with which we judge our parents. And it would be even worse, of course, to learn about carelessness and neglect that we've forgotten. The memory is destroyed or purified so that we can reinvent ourselves, start over, accuse, forgive, grow.

Like moviegoers who missed the first few minutes but stay for the next showing so as to understand the plot, we forget precisely the part of childhood that we later observe in our own children. They're the ones who remind us that we have forgotten, and then a new form of uncertainty emerges, one that can be shadowy and vertiginous but also stimulating and fertile. I think of that line by Paul Valéry: "Gaps are my starting point."

"For many years I claimed I could remember things seen at the time of my own birth," we read at the beginning of *Confessions of a Mask*, by Yukio Mishima, and in a way the whole novel emanates from that one superb sentence. Mishima's character chooses to believe in or invent an original and absolute autonomy, which beautifully exaggerates the idea, so dear to psychoanalysis, that we create our own memories.

That line gave me the idea for the Birth Project, which at first involved just asking my students to write about the day they were born. Later on, it evolved into an assignment that isn't original, but isn't all that common either: each student must go to the library and read the newspapers from the day they were born beginning to end, including horoscopes, movie and theater listings, obituaries, racing results, advertisements, etc. (There was always that one student who couldn't stop laughing about the maximum speed of computers in, say, 1996.)

The idea of the Birth Project is for everyone to imagine their mother paging through that same paper the morning her water broke and she had to head off to the hospital. It doesn't matter much what they write about, the exercise works because it triggers creative processes, allowing the teacher to be not a dictator of method or an absolute authority, but just an older colleague who knows the origin of the text and can usher along the writer's development.

Imagining the day of one's own birth foregrounds, with deceptive simplicity, the border between private and public. That's why I think this exercise is perfect for capturing, in the process, the enigma or game that is proposed or allowed for by the word *fiction*, so often misunderstood as merely a semiacademic synonym for *lie*. "I was born on a day / when God was sick, and / gravely so," says César Vallejo in a poem that would be funny to submit to a lie detector.

I've never applied the Birth Project to myself; I never wanted to materialize or maybe verify my conjectures about that day in 1975 that I always imagine in black and white, though the first photograph taken of me, when I was two weeks old, was in color. I'm not in many photos, maybe twenty out of the fifty or sixty total in our two family albums. The first one—which has a calm, inoffensive seascape on the cover—starts with my sister's birth in 1972, and its photos are nearly all black and white. In the second—whose cover shows a pair of blond lovers from behind as they watch the sunset—then-novel full-color photos predominate.

Thanks to conversations with his mother and to the diaries she wrote, the poet Robert Lowell, born in 1917, imagined in detail the time when, as he puts it, "America entered the war and my mother entered marriage." Then he adds this tender, precise bit of irony: "I was often glad I could not be blamed for anything that happened during the months when I was becoming alive." For me, when I was in my twenties and I'd page through our family photo albums, what I felt wasn't gladness but something like shame—at times directed at myself and at times toward others, but always overwhelming—not so much for what the pictures revealed, but for what I presumed they refused to show.

I don't remember having thought back then that those albums held too few photos—I think they may have even seemed abundant. I pictured my parents classifying those images on the adhesive pages during the most ferocious years of Pinochet's dictatorship. I felt like everything was too fragile and I was too stupid. It seemed horrible not to remember anything, or to recognize scenes implanted by family stories that always seemed vague to me, always overly individual.

"Remember when you were born?" I ask my son.

"Yeah. You picked me up and you were crying, but from joy."

He knows he doesn't remember and also that I know he doesn't remember, but every once in a while we play this game where we repeat a conversation about crying that we had when he was about eighteen months old—I was trying to explain to him that tears don't only mean sadness, because sometimes we cry from emotion. And then I got the idea to tell him about the day he was born, when I saw him for the first time just out of his mother's womb. I explained that when I first laid eyes on him I burst into tears, but from joy.

I have 1,422 photos on my phone, and my son appears in nearly every one of them. He was born 1,266 days ago, which means that I have taken, let's say, a photo for every day of his life. To that exorbitant collection we could add the pictures taken by his mother and his maternal grandmother and his photographer uncle . . . Suddenly, the possibility that someday he will have access to those photos and to the books his mother writes and the ones I write, books that feature him ever more frequently—and even if they don't, he is still there, lurking in the background—starts to feel unfair, and sometimes I think we should destroy those files to make room for a shiny new forgetting. And there's another, contradictory idea that also looms large, because lately I feel like I write for him, that I am my son's correspondent, that I'm writing dispatches to him live and direct from the time he will forget, from the erased years. Perhaps my writing has never been more justified than now, because in a way I'm writing the memories that he will lose. It's as if I were the secretary or nursery school teacher for some toddlers named Joe Brainard, Georges Perec, and Margo Glantz, and I wanted to facilitate the future writing of their *I Remember*s.

It's 1978 or 1979, I'm three or four years old, and I'm sitting on the sofa beside my father watching soccer on TV, when my mother comes in to refill our glasses of Coke. For decades I have considered this to be my first memory, and it doesn't, at first, seem suspect: I grew up in a family where not only my mother but all the women *waited on* men, and in a world where the TV was in the living room and was always turned on and almost always, for kids, permitted, same as Coke. This memory is not linked to any photograph or family story, and maybe that's why I considered it a pure, unimplanted, and unequivocal memory. Still, it's not hard to unravel that certainty: I'm sure that in the twenty years we lived under the same roof, my father and I watched a hundred or five hundred or one thousand soccer games together, and yet I remember this scene as something that happened only once.

I have the impression, and my father the certainty—as I've just confirmed, over the phone—that my passion for soccer didn't start so early; it came later, when I was six or seven and we were living in a different house in another city.

My memory does not assert, in any case, that we watched a whole game or that I was interested in soccer. It's just a flash that lasts two or three completely silent seconds. That silence, however, is perhaps the most suspicious thing about the memory, my father's silence in particular—he could watch the news stone-faced, but he was incapable of keeping quiet when he watched soccer. Even today, that's a difference between us: I watch games in a state of absolute tension with only the occasional comment, while my father shouts instructions and curses out the ref as if he could influence the game.

I think of the extraordinary beginning of Nabokov's *Speak, Memory*: the young "chronophobiac" who watches a home movie from before he was born and glimpses his mother, pregnant, and the waiting baby carriage that looks like a coffin to him. I think of Delmore Schwartz's devastating primal scream, "In Dreams Begin Responsibilities," one of the most beautiful stories I have ever read, or of the genius ravings of Vicente Huidobro in *Mío Cid Campeador*, or Laurence Sterne's in *Tristram Shandy*. I think of the chilling "invented memory" that gives shape to *The Tongue Set Free* by Elias Canetti. I think of certain fragments by Virginia Woolf and Rodrigo Fresán and Elena Garro. The list starts to seem endless, and I comb the shelves for books I want to reread—but suddenly

I notice that my son has been quiet for too long. I turn to see him sitting on the floor with his crayons. After several months spent drawing smoothies, he now specializes in pizzas and planets and pizza-planets.

My own first memory is not, on its surface, traumatic, but a cursory analysis is all it takes to find that in this film I am *exposed* to TV and to soccer and sexism and sugar and phosphoric acid, so that the memory acts as a foundation, and even, possibly, as a justification or an excuse. A more collective reading leads me to contrast that memory with period images: streets razed by military violence where some men and women resist with suicidal and idealistic courage—but not my father, who is watching a soccer game with me, or my mother, who is serving us Coke.

In my son's life, a "first memory" like mine would be impossible, because he has grown up in a world—or at least in a household—where no woman is at the service of any man, a world where it's his father who makes him breakfast every morning in a kitchen whose refrigerator does not hold Coca-Cola bottles. In fact, he has never tried Coke (not regular or Light or Zero) and he's also never seen a soccer game, because he has never watched TV, and these days soccer is played in empty stadiums.

I quit smoking and I drink very occasionally—though I still keep a small bar with bonsai-size bottles of wine, pisco, and mezcal—and I can go long periods without eating red meat or hormone-laced chicken, but, unfortunately, I have not been able to entirely break my addiction to Coke. I buy the occasional can, and my son watches curiously as I drink it, though he is sure that—as I tell him every time, with an insistence he will soon start to find fishy—it's medicine and it tastes terrible, to the point that when I finish drinking it, I put on a convincing show of gagging.

(My wife and I stack drafts of the poems, novels, or essays that we write on a side table next to the desk. My son recycles those sheets for his pizzas and planets. This morning he gave me a green-and-pink planet outlined with uneven skill, and I was surprised to find, on the back of it, these words: *I quit smoking and I drink very occasionally . . .*

I don't really like the person who wrote that paragraph. But that person was me. And I'm still me. I have a deep distrust of the satisfaction I feel at the thought that my wife and I are *doing it right*. I'm sure my parents also thought they were doing it right, and I myself think that some friends of ours, whose charming daughter watches TV and eats potato chips every day, are doing it quite well, maybe better than us. When it comes to parenting, in any case, the panic of getting it wrong is much more powerful than the desire to get it right. Along the same lines, I find that like so many other new parents, especially older ones, what I really want is not to *live better* but to *live longer*. Just not to die real soon, that's all.)

"Dad, when I was a baby, did the TV work?" my son asks me.

"I don't remember," I tell him. "I think so."

His whole life, he has believed that the TV in our bedroom is broken. We have shown him occasional videos on our phones (like *Yellow Submarine*, responsible for his hopefully incurable Beatlemania), and a few dozen photos, particularly ones from his first months of life. Hence his idea of *having been a baby*, which has consolidated in his mind the difference between a hazy, remote past and a past he remembers. Every time he meets a newborn he asks to see the photos, which to him are ancient, that depict the childhood of his childhood. Absorbed in the game of recognizing himself, he gazes at them in somber silence. I mention his silence because he is not a quiet person, not at all, but a conversationalist, a fabulist, a smooth talker.

As for his relationship to soccer, his desire to play was sudden. There was a time when he seemed absolutely uninterested, and considered the plush ball to be just another stuffed animal. The first time he saw me kick it he looked at me in surprise, but two seconds later he grabbed a poor stuffed zebra and kicked that too, and then he became an expert in the art of plush toy kicking. But for some months he still considered the ball a static toy, and although he'd occasionally give it a kick, as if to please me, it was much more common for him to talk to it and ask me to give it a voice.

Now we play every day, either in our small yard or recklessly in the living room, and he likes it a lot. Like all fathers I do my best to lose, to let him score on me. Being a father consists of letting your child win until the day when the defeat is real. Needless to say, if my son scores a goal that I genuinely wouldn't have been able to block, it's a double and undeniable satisfaction. And if I'm the one who by some miscalculation accidentally scores a goal, he immediately changes the rules and annuls my triumph. Sometimes he gets bored, not of playing, but of the game being exactly the way it is, and he adds some jigs and lurches that seem to me like folk dances from unknown countries.

There was a time when my son's most frequent act of vandalism was to appropriate the toilet paper to play a long series of unfathomable, quite abstract games. I've heard that most of the world's children share this penchant—if they were to publish their own magazine, full of searing reviews of uncomfortable diapers and fiery diatribes against weaning, I'm sure they would also dedicate several pages to toilet paper games, which would be something like their sports section.

"It's not toilet paper, Dad," he said one morning, getting out in front of my scolding. "It's *confort*."

Not long before, he had asked me why Chileans call toilet paper *confort*, which of course means *comfort*. My efforts to always talk to him using the most words possible (it's practically the only parenting strategy in which I've been truly consistent) led me into a very long digression about generic trademarks—I tried to use familiar examples like *Kleenex* or *crayon*—and about the curious cry of "There's no comfort!," which in and of itself sounds like a social or philosophical protest, but, when uttered by a Chilean, has a much more specific and urgent meaning. I don't know how much of that explanation my son understood, probably very little, but from that conversation arose the frequent joke of summoning each other using the phrase "There's no comfort!" and then clarifying: "There's no Confort comfort!"

My son went right on calling toilet paper *papel de baño*,

because he speaks Mexican—very Mexican—but I think on the morning in question he decided to say it in Chilean (his "father tongue") with the strategic intention of charming or distracting or disconcerting me.

"I know what I'm going to ask for from Viejito Pascuero," he told me, again in Chilean, using our term for *Santa Claus*.

"What?"

"A roll of comfort," he replied.

"Chilean?"

"Chilean or Mexican, I don't care. But I want one just for me."

It was August or September, a long time before Christmas, but in the following days I realized it wasn't a joke, that was his official request, and he made it through various channels. It was the only thing he wanted, a toilet paper roll of his own so we'd let him play in peace, in perfect and autonomous solitude. By December's end, however, when he was opening presents, his passion for toilet paper was already a thing of the past.

"That's what children are for—that their parents may not be bored," says a character of Ivan Turgenev's, and if the joke works it's because we tend to think of life with children, on the contrary, as an incessant daily sacrifice. Often, however, throughout the pandemic, I have momentarily relieved my anxiety or fury or melancholy by playing with my son, as if his existence functioned not only as a diversion, but also as an antidepressant or a tranquilizer.

Last week a dear friend called to tell me about his relapse into alcoholism and his uncontrollable Netflix marathons (his most frequent interaction with the world consisted of answering the question "Are you still watching?"), and of his constant fits of sadness caused by his abrupt baldness.

"I don't know how you guys do it," he told me suddenly, changing his tone or his rhythm.

"Do what?"

"I mean, with a kid."

How do *you* do it *without* a kid? I started to ask, but I didn't want to disillusion him: I was happy to know that in spite of everything, my friend felt or sensed that he was better off than us. There is something so definitive about fatherhood that until then I had never thought about what these months would have been like if I'd gone through them alone. Suddenly I found myself in a parallel world where I was, like my friend, an embittered alopecic, and it was very hard to imagine where the hell I would get the energy to fumble around in the sheets for the remote control (I was going to write "the energy to go on living," but it seemed too dramatic, though I'm sure that in that awful parallel world, the phrase would not have seemed dramatic at all).

"Onomatopoeia builds a world, sound gives color to ideas," writes David Wagner in *Speaks the Child*, an excellent book that I would like to quote in its entirety. I remember with a certain premature nostalgia how my son and I used to spend hours imitating the sounds of different animals—when our reper-

toire ran out, we would invent dog laughter, or horse tears, and
the game went on until we got joyfully lost in the nonsense:
a magpie yawn, a crocodile stammer, a possum sneeze.

Of all the lines of work involved in paternal care—stairwell
sherpa, wardrobe assistant, sock matcher, toy-litter collector,
lunchtime cheerleader, personal poolside lifeguard, etc.—
the one that I have performed with the greatest joy and, I
believe, skill, has been that of voice actor for all kinds of objects. Some of them are pretty typical—a lovely "transitional"
giraffe or some finger puppets who speak Spanish in a variety
of accents—and others a lot harder to anthropomorphize, like
the coffeepot, the windows, the guitar case, the omnipresent
thermometer, and even some objects that I consider disagree-
able from the outset, like the scale or—oh, how I hate it—the
pressure cooker.

Parenthood relegitimizes games that we gave up when our
sense of the ridiculous managed to take over everything—
even, sadly, our inner lives. I think of animism, a belief system
I never completely abandoned, but which now, in my son's
company, strikes me as not only fun but necessary. I really like
that scene in *Chungking Express*, the film by Wong Kar-wai,
when a character talks to a giant stuffed Garfield: I like it
because it's comic and serious at the same time; because it's
kitsch, like life, and because it's tragic, like life.

"How was school?" we asked our son with guilty eagerness,
when he'd been going for only a few days and there were still
some months before the pandemic broke out.

"Miss Mónica died," he replied.

"And Miss Patricia?"

"She died too."

"And the kids?"

"The kids ended." His tone was an attempt to be objective or truly newsy, but it came out as unintentionally sweet.

His newly acquired idea of death originated from the sight of a wilted flower in the yard. I wonder how that idea has changed since then, over the course of these months; I wonder again, over and over, unable to escape the question's gravity, what my son will remember of all this. I imagine him fifteen or thirty years from now, going through a hard drive of multitudinous terabytes, to find the ones that document his amnesiac phase. And maybe I prefer to imagine that he'll never see those photos, that he'll never read our books, that he'll never read this essay. I imagine him free to judge us harshly, to see us as savages who frittered away the planet, or maybe as the worst kind of cowards—those who believe themselves brave. Maybe I would rather imagine this adult of the future loving us the way I love my own parents: unconditionally, and with the fervent and probably doomed desire to never be like them.

"Memory is organized not from the past or from the present, but rather from the future," conjectures the psychoanalyst Néstor Braunstein in *Memory and Fear*, his fascinating book about first memories in literature. He adds: "What a person comes to be is not the result, but rather, on the contrary, the cause of memory."

A short wooden bridge that I crossed a thousand and one times; my mother, with the look of a mischievous little girl, plucking a newly ripened tomato from the vine, wiping it on her blouse, and taking a bite; an upright piano that belonged to the landlords of the house we lived in and thus remained permanently closed, though I snuck my hand in to get a sound from the keys; one morning when I jumped with feigned indolence on a bed that had just been peed on (by me); riding a tricycle with my sister, and the absurd and defiant fun of squashing the grapes on the ground under the arbor; the entertaining conversations through the fence with someone a little older than me who was named Danilo, and who defined himself as "a street kid." All these memories are tied to the same house in Villa Alemana where we lived in 1978 and 1979, and would work perfectly well as my first memory. Really, I don't think I have or have ever had any tools that would situate those moments along a timeline.

I feel like my son changes every day, and his fluctuations and accelerations have built the music that has allowed us to endure these months with joy. A few weeks ago he entered a bubble with five other children and a very patient teacher, and every morning he announces that he doesn't want to go, but he does go and he enjoys it; he needs those kids who don't play or dance to his rhythm, but who teach him something. They help each other, and together they walk away from their parents with happy tortoise steps.

I think Turgenev was right, and there is no contradiction: parents exist to amuse their children, and children are for keeping their parents from getting bored (or anxious). These are complementary ideas that perhaps could help us test out new definitions of happiness or love or physical exhaustion or all those things simultaneously. Right now, as I listen to the dire morning news on the radio, I miss my son's company—he usually gets up at six or even earlier, but now it's almost seven o'clock and he's still in bed and I want to wake him up, because I'm bored, because I'm anxious.

II.

The Kid with No Dad

"Dear motherfucking cocksucker of an asshole," writes Darío in his notebook, "I haven't heard from you in a few days, you fucking dickwad. I'm guessing someone threw a bag of poop and barf on you in the street, and you can't get rid of the smell of horse shit and sweaty socks, and on top of that you're farting out dick smell, you mangy mutt."

The letter is longer than that—it goes on for a full page, front and back. Darío reads it out loud, quite satisfied with the result. He doesn't talk like that, not at all: some of the kids at school even say derisively that he speaks *too good*, as though accusing him of something, as if an eleven-year-old boy were obliged to speak in nothing but curse words. And yet, he has now managed to write a letter that is utterly, brazenly indecent—it's an absolute triumph.

He seals the envelope with abundant saliva, runs eagerly to Sebastián's house, and throws the letter onto the flagstones leading up to the front door, emulating the mailman's technique. He goes home pleased, though it does occur to him that it might rain, and the letter that he worked so hard on could disintegrate on the ground. But rain isn't likely, not at all, it's more that he's uneasy and maybe even starting to feel regret—only now, with the letter already delivered, does he think of the terrifying possibility that Sebastián won't understand the game and will find the letter offensive or incomprehensible.

His friendship with Sebastián is the lucky silver lining of his fear of dogs—all dogs, in general, but specifically Simaldone, a tiny, vociferous blond mutt, woolly and mean, who had almost bitten his ankles five times. It was illogical and humiliating to take the long way home, but thanks to the detour Darío started running into Sebastián, who spent a couple of hours in his front yard every afternoon, lying in the sun in his giant sunglasses, even though summer was still a ways off, and some days, actually, it was cloudy and cold.

"Do you really not have a dad?"

Darío is not stupid or insensitive, but the first time he spoke to Sebastián, he blurted out that brutal question. It was the kind of thing that happened to him when he overrehearsed. He'd been wanting to talk to Sebastián for days, and he had decided to break the ice the way adults do, with some comment on the weather or music or soccer. But at the moment of truth he got nervous and blurted out that unfortunate question, which was at least honest, because around the neighborhood almost no one knew Sebastián's name, they all called him *the kid with no dad*. More than a nickname, of course, it was a condition they acknowledged in a low voice, in the tone of someone talking about a shameful or deadly illness that was maybe also contagious: a stigma based solely on the fact that Sebastián and his mother were the only inhabitants of their house. No one knew the details of their story.

"Yeah, more or less. I don't know my dad," Sebastián replied in an unconcerned tone, as if he were in fact answering a question about the forecast or a rock band or a soccer player. "He must be around somewhere, but I don't know him and I don't want to. There are some people it's better never to meet. I might just end up disappointed."

Darío was shocked. He wanted to know everything, he always did, but he could only think of more stupid questions.

"Have you seen pictures of your dad?" he finally asked.

"Yeah. Five or six."

"Do you look like him?"

"I guess. He has the same pointy nose as me. And I think he has green eyes too, but I'm not sure, because the photos are black and white."

Sebastián looked focused, thoughtful.

"You sure like to sunbathe," Darío observed, a few seconds later, to change the subject.

"I don't like to sunbathe."

"But you're out here lying in the grass every day, sunbathing."

"That's not true. I'm not sunbathing, I'm looking at the sky. At the clouds, mostly."

I'm not sunbathing, I'm looking at the sky, Darío repeated mentally. He thought he would remember that sentence.

"But there are almost no clouds."

"Still, I like the few that are there."

It was a cold afternoon, with clouds that were, in effect, scant but playful, as though they'd been sketched quickly, out of necessity or to combat boredom. Sebastián spoke with the singsong voice of a wise adult, though occasionally he would burst into shy, self-conscious laughter.

"And do they look dark like that?"

"Yeah. I like dark clouds better."

Sebastián took off his sunglasses and handed them to Darío with superstitious care, as if maneuvering a pair of delicate binoculars or a heavy tray of crystalware. Darío looked at the sky and tried to see what Sebastián saw. And he thought he did. It was the first time he tried to see the world through someone else's eyes. Through their eyes and their eyeglasses. The two of them sat in an odd synchronized silence, as if taking turns breathing, Sebastián inhaling when Darío exhaled.

"Have you ever been on a plane?" asked Sebastián.

"No."

"It's exciting to fly through the clouds. You feel like you're about to crash, but then nothing happens. Sometimes the plane shakes a little, but nothing happens."

"Where did you go?"

"Nowhere, but people have told me. Lots of people. Every time I meet someone who's been in a plane, I ask them if they've crashed into clouds."

"I bet it's really exciting. Both things."

"Both what things?"

"Flying in a plane and crashing through clouds."

"Yeah, like when you're riding in a car through the fog and it keeps you from seeing the road."

"Let's go in your house," Darío said.

"What for?" asked Sebastián.

"I need to go to the bathroom."

"Just pee in the bushes."

"I need to poop."

"Go to your own house!"

Darío insisted, saying he couldn't make it to his house. It wasn't true, he didn't need to go at all, he just wanted to see inside Sebastián's house. He liked to look at other people's houses, though they were all pretty much the same. Maybe that's why he liked it—every detail, every slight variation, led him to a long list of conclusions: the presence or absence of albums, of crucifixes, prayer cards, guitars, decorative bottles, encyclopedias, or traditional handicrafts.

Locked in Sebastián's bathroom, the first thing he did was inspect the medicine cabinet. He loved finding weird medications with funny names, but there was nothing but hair gel, cotton, and a giant bottle of iodine. Then he turned to the bathtub and still saw nothing very unusual or revealing: the same shampoo and the same conditioner everyone in the neighborhood used. When he came out of the bathroom, however, he discovered something astonishing: Sebastián had the main bedroom, and his mother had the smaller one. That a child would sleep in the best room in the house and his mother would settle for the worst one challenged almost everything Darío knew or thought he knew about the world.

"I don't think it's that weird," said Sebastián when Darío mentioned it. "I have a lot of stuff, and my mom barely has anything."

And maybe that was true, because Sebastián's room was full of boxes and toys, among them five prominently displayed Transformers, including Optimus Prime himself. (Darío had a Transformer too, but just a very secondary character, who only appeared in one episode of the whole series.) Darío thought that Sebastián's mother spoiled him, which in a way proved that the misfortune of not having a father also had its advantages. While they shared a yogurt in the kitchen, Darío thought about how being fatherless was pretty insignificant compared with the absolute tragedy of not having a mother.

"What time does your mom get home?" he asked.

"She always gets home late," said Sebastián. "She has a lot of work. She's a secretary."

Almost immediately, as if to prove him wrong, Lali walked in. Darío had seen her often in church, sitting beside Sebastián in the back pews, and lately he also saw her in the street, on her way home from work wearing the same uniform as now, small and a little hunched over. She walked fast, focused on the sidewalk, maybe because she didn't want to speak to anyone—or because she knew no one was going to speak to her, thought Darío. Now she greeted Darío familiarly, as if she were used to finding him there, or to her son having friends over. Before locking herself into the small room, her bedroom, Lali served them up some generous, exaggerated portions of Neapolitan ice cream, all three flavors for Darío and only two for Sebastián.

"I'm against chocolate ice cream," explained Sebastián.

"You don't like chocolate?"

"Sure, I do, who doesn't like chocolate? But I don't like it as ice cream. Chocolate is warm, it's crazy to make ice cream out of it. It's like a contradiction."

The boys argued passionately about chocolate ice cream, and they also discussed vanilla and strawberry ice cream for an improbably long time, as if they were political activists deciding on the future of the country, though at times they also seemed like radio personalities filling up airtime. When Darío was leaving he saw Lali, in a nightgown now, with the headphones of an immense Walkman over her ears. Darío associated Walkmans with young people, and he had never seen an adult person, much less someone's mother, wearing headphones.

II.

Darío and Sebastián immediately became inseparable. They met up every day, Monday through Sunday, and they didn't need to make plans: Darío showed up at five, sometimes earlier, and they almost always stretched out to watch the clouds and classify them according to a complicated system Sebastián had invented. But they also talked about all kinds of things or took penalties or sprayed each other with the garden hose. Occasionally, toward the end of the day, Darío would meet up with his other friends, who now eyed him suspiciously. One indiscreet girl told him that behind his back people called him "the kid without a dad's friend." He didn't care, or not much.

One day Darío and Sebastián happened to run into each other at the bus stop as they were both coming back from their respective schools. They marveled at the coincidence, which was a normal, even predictable one, but to them it seemed like a sophisticated magic spell.

"Should we go to your house? I've never been," said Sebastián.

Darío, the consummate tourist of other people's houses, didn't especially like to show off his own, but he was pleased at the sudden and romantic thought that this would bring his friendship with Sebastián to the next level.

"But let's go by your house first," said Darío.

"What for?"

He didn't know what to say. All Darío wanted was to avoid the short way home, which was the natural route from the bus stop to his house. He felt a dire anxiety at the thought of facing Simaldone again; his legs gave out a little more with each step and he felt like he was going to faint, so he decided to start walking faster just to get the torturous scene over with. Sebastián sped up too, thinking it was a game. Against all odds, the hell-raising mutt greeted them calmly, as if it had been waiting for them, or more precisely waiting for Sebastián, because it didn't even seem to notice Darío was there. Sebastián stopped to pet the dog, who thanked him by licking his face. Darío couldn't believe it.

"Have you ever had a dog?"

"No, but I like them."

Darío almost revealed to his friend that he was afraid of them, but in the end he kept quiet, of course.

That afternoon they had charquicán for lunch and played Atari and guitar (Sebastián didn't know how to play, but managed a pretty good A note for a beginner).

"That was really fun," Sebastián said as he was leaving. "I like your house, but mine's better."

It was a kind of joke, which Darío didn't get and would later recall obsessively, because precisely that day, with no warning or notice, Sebastián disappeared. At first Darío rang his doorbell every day, but no one ever answered, and then he became absolutely certain that both Sebastián and Lali were home but didn't want to let him in. There was no reason to think so, but Darío couldn't let go of that pesky idea. And that was when, a little bored but also a little worried, he wrote that letter full of curse words.

III.

The letter, now yellowed by the elements, has spent two weeks in the front yard. Darío's leading hypothesis is that Sebastián met his father and he and his mom went off to live with him somewhere else, maybe in another country. But he also has other theories that are less precise and more unsettling, some of them even supernatural. At last, one morning he goes outside and finds, nestled in the bougainvilleas of his own front yard, Sebastián's glorious reply, and its humor and vulgarity equal or surpass those of the original letter. He is moved to find that his dear friend understood the game to perfection. And he likes Sebastián's handwriting, he thinks it's original, with its odd mixture of upper- and lowercase, print and cursive letters.

"Why'd you disappear for so long?" Darío asks that same afternoon, very seriously, though he tries to sound unconcerned.

"I was hiding from a motherfucking cocksucking son of a bitch with a snotty dickface who smells like ass crack," replies Sebastián.

The laughter seems like it will never end, like an earthquake with many aftershocks, but little by little the silence gains ground and Darío asks again—he wants to know the truth. Sebastián explains that he and his mother had to go to Quillota to take care of his sick grandmother.

"Is she better now?"

"She died."

Sebastián doesn't seem sad, and maybe that's why Darío thinks it's a lie, a joke, and in fact he almost starts laughing. But then, a few seconds later, he is able to find or focus in on the sadness in his friend's face. No one in Darío's family has ever died, and his rudimentary concept of death is limited to the disappearance of his cat, Speedy, many years ago now—he doesn't even remember Speedy that well.

"I think it's missing some pieces, I haven't played in a long time," says Sebastián in the living room of his house, as they're setting up the Monopoly board.

"I don't feel like playing anyway," says Darío. "Tell me about your grandma."

"I don't want to," replies Sebastián. "That's why I want to play, so I won't think about her. She hated this game."

"Why?"

"Because it's a shitty game made for bloodsucking capitalists."

"Let's not play, then."

"No, let's play, just to have something to do. I'll start crying if I talk about her."

In the end they don't play, they lie on the bed and watch episodes of *I Dream of Jeannie* and *Bewitched* while Darío thinks about Sebastián's sadness and tries to imagine life without his grandmother. That is, without his maternal grandmother, and also without a father and as such without a paternal grandmother. He asks Sebastián for a notebook and starts to write another letter. Sebastián immediately starts writing one too, and when they finish they read the letters in low voices and roll with laughter. It becomes a regular game: two or three times a week they write letters together, side by side at the dining-room table, in a kind of ongoing literary workshop.

In real life their relationship is harmonious, while those letters project a parallel world where the boys are a couple of compulsive shit talkers who never see each other but who reproach each other for all kinds of slights.

"Let's go out and wander aimlessly," Darío sometimes suggests. He loves that hyperbolic phrase, and uses it all the time.

He feels safe walking with Sebastián, who inspires unanimous respect in dogs. But not just respect—what Sebastián inspires in dogs, Darío thinks, is true devotion; even the meanest barkers just gaze up at him in adoration. Over the course of those walks, however, Sebastián often starts to feel guilty, since his mom forbids him from going beyond the six or seven blocks of the neighborhood. It's not that Darío is necessarily allowed to go any farther; it's just one of the many gray areas in his childhood contract.

"I don't like to lie to my mom," admits Sebastián at the end of one almost-summer afternoon.

Suddenly they actually are a little lost amid a strange landscape of factories and auto repair shops. A man riding a front-load tricycle points them toward their neighborhood.

"Your mom will never find out. Why does she give you so many rules, anyway?"

"Because I'm all she has."

"Right."

They're silent during a red light that seems particularly long. They've been walking for a while and they're still not sure they are going in the right direction. They are relieved when they recognize a long line of plum trees and then the arcade where they sometimes play foosball. They're in a hurry, but they play a quick game anyway.

"That's why some people have two kids, or lots of kids," says Sebastián. "If one of them dies on you, you have another, and so on. You can't kill yourself, no matter how sad you are."

"And what about if I die?" asks Darío right as he scores a goal with a spinning shot.

"Well, there are still three of you. If you die, your parents won't kill themselves. They'll be pretty sad for the rest of their lives thinking about their dead son, looking at photos and stuff, but they won't kill themselves. But if I died, my mom would be all alone. I don't think she could take it, she'd shoot herself."

They get home a few minutes before Lali. She makes them some vanilla milk and then turns on her Walkman. With the echoes of their earlier conversation still tingling in his head, Darío thinks that Lali must still be sad about her mother's death, although really what he thinks is that Lali has always been sad, that she is a sad person. And that the music she listens to, as such, must be sad. He asks Sebastián what kind of music his mom listens to, but Sebastián says he doesn't really know. Darío tries to get close enough to Lali to solve the enigma, but she apparently listens to music at a reasonable volume, and since she doesn't move her head or any other body part to the beat, Darío comes to think that actually the Walkman is off and she's only wearing the headphones to create a sort of force field around herself.

"What kind of music do you listen to?" he asks her directly, boldly.

"Where's Seba?"

"In the bathroom," Darío replies.

Lali sits on the sofa as if she needed time to respond to the question.

"Do you want to know what I'm listening to now, or what kind of music I like in general?"

"Both."

"Tangos, now. But I don't really like them. I'm listening because my mom liked them. I gave her this tape for her birthday one year. When I was young I liked the Bee Gees. Well, I'm still young. And I still like the Bee Gees. Of the newer stuff I like REO Speedwagon and Debbie Gibson."

I'm still young. Darío mulls over Lali's possible youth. No father or mother could ever seem young to him.

IV.

The friends don't see each other as much over Christmas and New Year's, and in January Darío goes on vacation to Loncura and Sebastián is alone, probably resigned to watching the sky under the blazing sun of the brutal Santiago summer. Darío likes the beach—who doesn't?—but he doesn't love having his parents hovering around him all day long, so desperate to have fun. He misses Sebastián, a lot. As often happens at the coast, the days are stifling, almost cold, with slow, copious clouds that barely let the sun through. It's a little funny or pitiful to see the obstinate vacationers staking their useless umbrellas in the sand.

There's a yellow pay phone near their rented cabin. Darío thinks it would be cool if he could call Sebastián, but

Sebastián's house doesn't have a phone. Neither does Darío's—they live in a world that is still phone-free. In the afternoons he lurks at a certain distance from the phone, listening to other people's calls. The connections are almost always bad, and people shout sentences that are very private, sometimes ludicrous, and Darío tries to remember them so he can write them later in his notebook: *I contributed half but it's not for that; of course I know that he's family; let him walk home like always.*

One night he stays up late in a full-on epistolary trance. He produces a brilliant, extremely vulgar letter, and he's almost positive it's the best of his abundant oeuvre. Although his plan is to give it to Sebastián when he gets home, he takes advantage of an outing to Quintero to go to the post office and send it by registered mail. Luckily he remembers the number on the front of Sebastián's house. That same day he finally convinces his parents to buy him some sunglasses that are very much like his friend's. During his last weeks at the beach, Darío spends hours lying in the sand wearing his brand-new sunglasses. And he even comes up with new cloud classifications while he thinks intently about the wonderful scene of the mailman delivering the letter to Sebastián.

Back in Santiago, the first thing he does is go over to see his friend. It's early, and he figures Sebastián must be at home watching TV. But no one is there, or at least no one comes to the door, and Darío thinks he has disappeared again. He stays there at the door like a security guard, waiting, and he's still there when Lali gets home from work. She seems uncomfortable. Darío's suspicion or premonition is true this time: Lali tells him Sebastián is busy, that he's been busy all day and she ordered him not to open the door, because the two of them cannot be friends anymore. She won't give him any explanation. Darío protests, and she leaves him there talking to himself.

He goes home devastated, kicking a pebble in front of him. The next day he finds a short letter from Sebastián, with no cursing. It's a breakup letter, a resignation from the friendship. Sebastián doesn't explain very well, but Darío understands that Lali read the letters and misinterpreted everything. Darío spends hours speculating; he doesn't know if she read all the letters or only one, which of course doesn't matter at all.

Darío is insistent by nature, but Sebastián won't open the door. Darío intercepts Lali again, and she again forbids him from coming over anymore. As a last resort, he writes a letter to his friend's mother. It is the most florid and eloquent and neatly written letter he has composed in his life, the only one born of an urgent desire to obtain something concrete, the only one fully dedicated to apologizing. He is hopeful, he really believes that everything will work out, but weeks pass and no answer comes. "It was a game, Lali, a game, just a game." Many nights he lies awake whispering those words with rage.

The few times they run into each other in the street, Sebastián looks down and speeds up. Maybe he has also suffered or is suffering now, but Darío thinks it sure doesn't show, and he tries to dislike Sebastián. He remembers their conversation about death, but he doesn't want to feel compassion, he wants to despise his friend. He decides that Lali is an old prude and that Sebastián's obedience is incomprehensible—she would never find out if they kept being friends. But Sebastián obeys her, fears her. Darío feels like he could come to hate Sebastián, but he misses him. And he misses Lali, too.

Darío tries to go out as little as possible. For now he is trapped, there seems to be no solution: when he takes the long way home he is upset by passing his ex-friend's house, and when he takes the short way it's disastrous, because Simaldone's hatred seems to have multiplied a thousandfold. "Dogs can smell fear," Darío tells himself, sometimes out loud—people have told him that his whole life. He repeats it like a mantra, to psych himself up, but it doesn't work at all.

He manages to miss a whole week of school by inventing successive illnesses. When they finally take him to the doctor, it turns out he really is sick. He is diagnosed with a new disease, one that has just been discovered, says the doctor: irritable bowel syndrome. But he still has to go back to school. And Darío refuses. Even his parents, who tend to ignore problems, realize that something more is going on. They interrogate him clumsily until he has no choice but to confess his fear of Simaldone. His mother tells him to just take the long way home, but his father, after laughing his head off, declares that solution to be sissyish and stupid: real men face their fears. Darío insists that he's only afraid of that one dog, though eventually he is forced to admit that he fears all the dogs in the world.

One night, Darío's dad decides to talk to Simaldone's owners. It's a rare occurrence: Darío's parents don't usually talk to the neighbors. Adults, in general, don't talk to each other; it's the kids who spend the whole day in the street, like island emissaries, or traders on an archipelago. Darío's father tells Simaldone's owners that they can't let the dog run loose all the time. Simaldone's owners say that the dog is a little grouchy, sure, but he guards their house and by extension the whole neighborhood, that he's a valiant dog. And anyway, he only barks at car tires and people who are unfamiliar or suspicious. Perhaps, they insinuate, the dog finds Darío, for some reason, to be a perpetually unfamiliar or suspicious person. That isn't exactly true either, because Simaldone barks at almost everyone, but the argument works and is established almost as truth. Toward the end of that impromptu meeting, Simaldone himself, panting amicably, comes over to Darío's dad, who pets him and shakes his right paw as though sealing an agreement.

"You have to face your fears," his father tells him later. Carefully uttered, the phrase could have sounded tender and even protective, but he says it harshly, as if stating a decree, as if forbidding fear forever. Darío doesn't want his father to defend him from anything, doesn't want his father to ever go talk to any of the neighbors again, so he tries, every day, to get used to that cynical bully of a dog: he tortures himself by walking more slowly, as if he really wanted the mutt to attack him. Every once in a while he stops and looks the dog in the eyes, and the dog barks at him louder, maybe a little disconcerted but still intimidating. And maybe Darío does wish for exactly that: for Simaldone to chomp on his ankle and prove him right to everyone, even if he has to spend the rest of his life on crutches.

V.

Two years pass, full of defining events. The feeling of change is breathtaking, dizzying: Darío has just turned thirteen, he is officially tall and thin, and a few constellations of hateful zits cartoonishly advertise that he is in fact a teenager. Now he goes to a school far away from the neighborhood and in the afternoon session, which at first he didn't like because it all felt backward, but he's come to enjoy getting up past nine and eating breakfast alone in his room with the music on full blast.

He has just left his house to head to class, and he walks with quick and confident steps, for what had once seemed impossible has now come to pass: Simaldone no longer barks at Darío, just growls occasionally at the sight of him. Despite the gray fur around his snout, Simaldone is still a young dog, passionately dedicated to barking at car tires and also at some people, especially children, but he has finally left Darío alone, maybe for good.

Darío reaches the bus stop and is annoyed to find that no one else is waiting. When the drivers see a solitary kid in a school uniform, they often just drive right past, pompous and resolute, so Darío feels ridiculous standing there like a beggar. He contorts his face muscles and holds his breath, hoping to create some impression of adultness. It's a laughable strategy that today, however, seems to work—he sees the approaching bus slow down and he prepares for a triumphant entrance, even starting in on a broad smile to flash the driver, but just then he feels a rock hit his back. When he turns around he sees a snot-nosed boy of about seven years old staring at him defiantly.

"What's your problem, you little turd?" he asks with contempt that still sounds sympathetic.

"What's *your* problem, motherfucker?" the kid retorts, his

voice very shrill even for such a young child. "Go on, get on your bus, fucking coward."

"How dare you talk to me like that, you little birdbrain?" Darío resigns himself to missing the bus, and maybe it's because of that hesitation that he comes up with such a strange insult, comical really—his grandmother used to call him that sometimes, affectionately: birdbrain.

"What're you messing with my kid brother for, fucking spaz, you want us to kick the living shit out of you, fucking cheesedick?" chimes in the aggressor's older brother, who had been observing the scene from behind a tree. He is maybe fifteen years old, definitely older than Darío, and he's a few centimeters shorter but much burlier—a full-fledged bruiser.

"Your brother threw a rock at me."

Darío's words sound naive; he still hasn't understood this is an ambush.

Then something happens that is beautiful, in a way. The bully takes out a tissue and wipes his little brother's nose. For some seconds, while he contemplates this fraternal scene, Darío entertains the hope that it will all end there, at big talk and bluster. He has never been in a fight and no one has ever hit him, not counting his mother's sporadic slaps.

"Get on the ground, butt munch," the bully orders him. "Nicky, go on and beat the shit out of him. All by yourself, just like I taught you, and if he tries to fight back, I swear I'll clobber him."

Darío obeys. The kid looks more excited than enraged— they have clearly planned this. Nicky kicks Darío in the legs, laughing his head off; Darío covers his balls to at least soften the blows. Nicky's brother cheers after every kick as if he were witnessing a fireworks display, or, more precisely, as if he had organized the display himself and was now proudly taking in his masterpiece.

The beating is long and convoluted and even somehow tedious. At one point, as if they were at the beach playing in the sand, Nicky throws a handful of dirt in Darío's eyes, and it forms a thick mud as it mixes with the tears that are just starting to well up. He keeps his eyes closed for several minutes while Nicky goes on kicking him in the legs and ass. A few passersby simply skirt around the fight, like superstitious people avoiding a ladder. Darío hears their footsteps, their voices, and feels humiliated. Nicky and his brother force him to stand up and walk to a small park, or to something that in the future should become a park but for now is just a patch of stubbly grass.

"Get on the ground again, chucklefuck. Go on, Nicky, you're doing great, champ."

Nicky kicks him three times in the face, and Darío feels the blood flow from his left cheek and mix with the tearful mud. He manages to grab the kid's ankles and knock him to the ground, but the bully immediately comes to his brother's aid and punishes Darío with a formidable kick to the ribs, and once he's immobilized again the bully does something unexpected: he takes off Darío's shoes and starts hitting him in the head like he's trying to kill flies. Then Nicky and the bully go through Darío's backpack and find the cheese sandwich he'd packed for lunch, which they greedily devour. Darío tries to console himself with the thought that they are poor and hungry, though he's not so sure about that. Before leaving, they also take his jacket.

Darío doesn't pass out, but he has trouble moving. He hears more voices and footsteps, the noise of cars and buses going by. It's ludicrous that no one comes to his aid. He thinks he feels something like the blossoming of bruises all over his body. They are future bruises, of course, but he thinks he can feel them already, inscribed and inevitable. He takes off his shirt and uses it to stem the blood on his face.

VI.

"Can you walk?" someone asks him: Sebastián.

Sebastián's voice has changed, but Darío recognizes it immediately. When he connects those words with his ex-friend's face, he feels a mixture of gratitude and panic. While he confusedly explains that he has to get to school but can't go in this condition, he focuses on Sebastián's incipient mustache, still unhardened by the first shave.

He holds out hope of finding his backpack, but the bullies took everything. He removes his socks and leans against Sebastián to walk. They're an odd pair: Sebastián is coming back from the Catholic school he still attends, his tie just a little loosened and his uniform impeccable—even his shoes look freshly shined—while Darío walks barefoot and wounded with his bloody shirt balled up in his hand.

"I can't go to my house," he says then.

"Why not?"

"I don't want anyone to see me like this," he says.

"Then we'll go to mine," says Sebastián.

It's a fast-cloud afternoon: two or three tufts have set off on a kind of race whose prize seems to be fusing with another, larger cloud. But neither of them looks at the sky the way they used to; instead they watch the ground and step carefully. They walk the two blocks to Sebastián's house, passing neighbors who shoot them sidelong glances. Only one woman offers to help, but Sebastián answers for both of them, with a smile, that there's no cause for concern, everything is under control. Darío makes a huge effort to walk a little faster. His whole body hurts, but he isn't thinking about the pain or what has just happened, he is thinking about Sebastián, about the strange circumstance of leaning on his ex-friend or his recovered friend.

Once they're in his house, Sebastián takes care of cleaning Darío's wounds with iodine ("Is it the same bottle as before?" Darío wonders), then turns on the shower. While the warm water falls over his body Darío thinks how Sebastián knows just what to do, as if this were his job. Then he thinks that Sebastián is simply more used to being home alone, and maybe, because of that, is more prepared for life.

His pants are dirty but not torn. His shirt, on the other hand, is stained and ripped and can only be thrown in the trash. Sebastián hands him a peach-colored T-shirt and some old sneakers. The T-shirt fits; Darío is taller than Sebastián now, but they still wear the same size. Sebastián gives Darío an aspirin for the pain and then leads him to his room, which is no longer the main bedroom, but the smaller one.

"We switched," Sebastián explains, before Darío can ask.

"You don't have so much stuff anymore," says Darío, just to say something.

Sebastián shrugs and goes to the kitchen, and Darío is left alone in this room that seems like an imitation of the previous one, though perhaps an imitation that is more reasonable or genuine. He tries to put on his grimy pants, but his entire body aches, so he lies on the bed in his underwear. He sleeps for ten minutes, but when he wakes up he thinks hours have

passed. It's not cold, but Sebastián has put a blanket over
him. There's a glass of cold milk on the nightstand, and he
gulps it down in two long swallows.

"Wanna watch a movie?"

"What movie?"

"I've got a lot," says Sebastián.

"But you've seen them all already."

"But maybe you haven't. And I can watch them again."

"I dunno. How've you been?"

Darío's question is a natural one, but it sounds forced or
sad. Maybe that's why Sebastián merely smiles. A long silence falls over them, and it weighs on Darío. It isn't a tense
silence, in any case. It's different from the silence that reigns
in his house or the silence of mass or the silence during tests
at school. Nor is it like the silence of before, when they used
to look at clouds or write their foulmouthed letters, but maybe
it is, maybe it's a little like the silence of back then.

Sebastián leaves the room and comes back with a boom
box and puts on a tape, *The Head on the Door* by the Cure,
very quietly. Darío only knows the first song, and he mentally hums along. The music lulls him: he wakes up when
side A ends. Sebastián is in a chair, looking at him. Darío
thinks or rather knows that his unexpected host has been
there for a while. Sebastián gets up to flip the tape over.

Darío feels better. Still lethargic, but better. He curls up in
bed like someone hitting the snooze button for another ten
minutes. He can just picture his dad, angrily telling him to
learn how to defend himself. And he thinks he does know
how to defend himself; he thinks that he has always, somehow, known how to defend himself. Then he remembers the

bully wiping his little brother's nose, and he replays the scene in his head again and again. He imagines himself wiping the nose of a nonexistent little brother, or that he is the little brother and a giant big brother is wiping his nose. He thinks that maybe it was just a lesson: maybe Nicky gets beaten up at school and his older brother decided to teach him to defend himself using that senseless and bloodthirsty method. He lies unmoving in that bed that isn't his, feeling the sheet scratching his legs; suddenly, all the pain he feels in his body seems to come from that scratchy sheet.

That's when Lali comes home. He's afraid to face her, to see her again. He hears her and Sebastián talking. He can't make out what they are saying, but there's no yelling, there doesn't seem to be a disagreement.

"Do you feel like you can get up?" Lali asks in a casual, untroubled tone, a few minutes later.

Darío nods. She helps him to his feet and the two of them sit at the table.

"Where's Sebastián?"

"I sent him out for supplies. How are you?"

"Okay," says Darío, disoriented and nervous.

"A little worse for the wear, I'd say," says Lali.

"So where are you working now?" Darío has noticed that Lali's uniform is different, and he uses that detail to change the subject.

"What's it to you, ya nosy brat?"

Lali says this with false aggression—sweetly, rather.

"Sorry," says Darío.

"I work at the same place as always."

"So they just changed the uniform."

"Yep," replies Lali. "How about you, do you still speak only in curse words?"

"No," says Darío. "I hardly ever use them. Only when I'm really mad. And sometimes I get mad and I don't even swear. But I hardly ever get mad. I'm a good kid."

Darío speaks in the exact tone of someone alleging their innocence. Lali looks at him tenderly.

"I was taught that children shouldn't curse," she says. "But sometimes I think I was taught all wrong. Or I learned all wrong."

Although it is an apology, it sounds like she's thinking out loud. Darío feels an eager relief.

"It was just a game," he says in a tiny voice.

He immediately regrets that unnecessary sentence. She bites a nail, two nails.

"I bite my nails too," says Darío.

"It's bad for you," says Lali. "Really bad."

Sebastián comes back with a small mille-feuille cake. He is out of breath, as if he had run to the bakery and back. Between the three of them, they set the table and cut the cake. Suddenly they're like a family, Darío thinks. Or else he feels like a distant cousin who dropped in at dinnertime, no warning or explanation. I don't really know them, I never really did, Darío thinks then. But I'll get to know them now, maybe.

"We're pretty poor in this house, but we eat cake every day," says Lali.

Then she asks Darío to tell his story.

Darío tries to tell everything, in detail, though at times he feels like he's making it up and he stumbles. Lately, he always has this feeling that he's making everything or almost everything up. But now something has happened to him, something real, something serious, something worth telling.

"You were assaulted, kiddo, you were mugged. It happens to the best of us," says Lali.

"They didn't mug me."

"They stole your backpack, your jacket, and your shoes," says Sebastián, who had been silent up till then. "They mugged you!"

"They only took that stuff because they could. But they weren't muggers. They just wanted to beat me up."

"They wanted to rob you, that's why they beat you up."

"Were they hoodlums?" Lali asks.

"No," says Darío. "They were normal kids, like us."

"But you boys wouldn't do anything like that," says Lali.

"No," says Darío.

"No," says Sebastián.

"So you two are the good guys."

"Yeah," says Darío, hesitant.

Maybe Sebastián and his mother are right and those kids simply wanted to rob him. He thinks that from now on he's going to tell the story as an assault, because an assault is more logical, less humiliating. They're on their second slices of cake. Sebastián gets up to bring the boom box over and puts the tape back on. Lali hums the first song, and Darío thinks that maybe the tape is hers, that maybe she likes the Cure. Or they both do. He likes to imagine such a thing, mother and son listening to and enjoying the same music. He also thinks that Sebastián doesn't talk much and no longer says the kind of clever things he used to say. He's changed. But maybe he hasn't changed. There's no way to know yet, I need time, thinks

Darío. Maybe later on, or tomorrow, or someday in the future, he'll seem like who he was two years ago.

"Dickie," Lali says suddenly, in the enthusiastic tone of someone finally managing to solve an extremely complicated enigma.

"What?" asks Darío.

"If the younger brother is named Nicky, maybe his older brother is named Dickie. Did he smell like a dick? Did he look like one?"

A peal of laughter swells, and it is freeing, very long, and contagious.

"I bet his name was Dickface," says Sebastián.

"Or Dumb Asshole," says Lali.

Darío smiles with a new, complete joy, while Sebastián and his mother go on for a long time venturing possible names for Nicky's brother: Twat Waffle, Flame Brain, Johnny Assclown, Douchecanoe, Alexander von Shitgibbon.

Skyscrapers

I didn't go to New York because I didn't want to cut my hair. And my father didn't read my "Letter to My Father."

"I'll read it next time I feel like crying," he told me. "Except I never feel like crying."

I didn't know how to respond. I never did know how to respond. That's why I wrote, that's why I write. What I write are answers I didn't think of in time. The drafts of those answers, actually.

The first time I tried to write this story, for example, I erased you. I thought it would be possible to conceal your absence, as if you simply hadn't shown up for that day's performance and we, the other actors, had to improvise at the last minute.

Only now do I realize that this story started with you. Because although I might prefer not to acknowledge it, this is, in every sense, a love story.

✦ ✦ ✦ ✦ ✦

Just a week earlier, everything had been fine. It would be wrong to say that things were good, because things were never truly good back then, but sometimes the status quo worked, and there were even happy days. My father and I in the car, windows rolled down, listening to the news: maybe we looked like friends, or brothers on our way to work, each pleased to have the other there to enliven the ride with small talk.

"You should learn to drive," my dad told me that morning, while we were stopped at a light.

I'd been hearing the same thing since I was fourteen years old, or maybe even longer, since I was twelve. Now, at twenty, I was thinking that yes, maybe it did make sense for me to learn how to drive, if only to cultivate the pleasant, stupid fantasy of a speedy escape down the highway after stealing everything my parents owned, starting with the car. But I also liked not knowing how to drive, the idea of never learning.

"I could learn, yeah," I said.

"You want me to teach you?" he asked eagerly. "Tomorrow? Or Sunday?"

"Tomorrow. Sounds great."

My dad's office was downtown, but he took a detour of several blocks to drop me off near the United States consulate, where I had a visa appointment. I was prepared for endless red tape, but I was out in an hour and even had time to make it to Schuster's class. I was only a little late, which wasn't a problem, because the professor hated formalities—students went in and out of the classroom without being excused, as if the session were being held in the street and we were merely the momentary audience of a preacher or a street vendor.

I ducked into the back row, as always, and took out my photocopied César Vallejo poems and the gigantic notebook where I jotted down random phrases. I didn't bother trying to take real notes—not even the most diligent students were able to capture the sometimes brilliant but always disconcerting soliloquies of Guillermo Schuster. I recall him mid-harangue, a Gitanes in his right hand and in his left a coffee cup, which wasn't, strictly speaking, a cup, but the lid of his thermos. Each sip marked another step up in the professor's crescendo: his performance began with general observations, halting but sound, and then veered off into loquacious digressions that ended in utter dispersal. There was a rumor that the thermos Schuster drank from so methodically during classes contained coffee spiked with whiskey or pisco, and there were even those who claimed it was an exclusive Polish vodka, straight, of course, since it would have been sinful to mix it with coffee.

"Could you please put out your cigarette, professor?" said an unfamiliar student that morning: you.

"Why?" Schuster asked, genuinely taken aback, as if he'd just heard something crazy.

"I'm pregnant," you replied.

These days it's hard to make people understand how smoking in classrooms was not only allowed back then, but was considered a completely normal, almost reasonable thing to do. Sometimes, even in the middle of winter with the windows closed, there could be five or more cigarettes lit at the same time; if you saw it in a movie, it would seem like an exaggeration, a gimmick, a parody.

I thought Schuster would react with infinite disdain and would turn, as always, to sarcasm, but instead he gave you a curious smile that lasted two or three seconds before he stamped his cigarette out on the floor. The T.A., who observed the class with the demeanor of a fan and often synchronized his own cigarettes with Schuster's, as if the two of them belonged to the same team of elite smokers, also had to put his out. And I had to fight my own desire to light up.

After class, the professor and his assistant headed quickly out to the parking lot, and I walked with them so I could tell them about my upcoming trip to New York.

"Don't worry about attendance, it's okay." Schuster rubbed his chin as though caressing a thick imaginary beard. "But I'm just not convinced by that city. I don't like New York."

"Why not?"

"It's overrated," he said, in his customary tone of a skeptical intellectual. "One of my kids lived there for three years, in Brooklyn."

"Terrible city, New York," the assistant said. "Just awful."

One of my kids, I thought, impressed that Schuster had more than one child. I could easily imagine him as someone's father, almost all the adults I knew had at least one child. But the thought that Schuster had *produced*—that was the verb I used—two or more human beings seemed to me, in that moment, strange or perhaps alarming.

I said goodbye to them and was about to light an overdue cigarette when I saw you approaching.

"Do you have another smoke?" you asked.

"I thought you were pregnant."

"Some pregnant women smoke," you told me. "No, the truth is that I just lost my baby. Just now, in the bathroom. It was horrible."

There was a short silence. You smoked faster than me.

"So why'd you tell him to put it out?"

"To fuck with him. He was just talking so much," you

said. "I've never been pregnant," you added, as if it were necessary to clarify.

"Did you like the class?"

"Yeah. I liked the poems we read. Vallejo is awesome. I didn't understand the professor at all, but I liked the class. Are they always like that?"

"Yeah. Schuster's pretty crazy."

I had to get to my Intro to Research Methodology class, but instead I decided to keep walking aimlessly with you. You told me you were thinking about majoring in literature, and you'd gone to Schuster's class out of curiosity.

"I never wanted to study anything," you said. "And I still don't know if I really want to."

We were both twenty years old, but you sounded more adult, or maybe it's more like I felt you were a sort of ancient and noble presence. That was when I really looked at you, and became aware of your almost disproportionately large eyes. I noticed your aquiline nose, your long, thin fingers, and your tiny, green-painted nails. Your hair was longish, but still shorter than mine. Mine reached my shoulders. You also reached my shoulders, but you struck me as one of those people who seem tall even though they aren't.

We walked together toward Plaza Ñuñoa. I tried to combat the silence, because I still hadn't discovered that it was possible, even necessary, to share silences. I told you about my trip to New York, and though I was trying to come off as nonchalant and worldly, I'm sure I sounded pretty arrogant— I should have practiced in front of the mirror first. You had already been to New York and much of Europe, and you'd lost count of how many times you'd been to Buenos Aires, your favorite city in the whole world. But you didn't tell me all that then. You just mentioned that you'd been to New York.

"What was your favorite thing about New York?"

"Some paintings by Paul Klee. At the Met. Those were the best. It wasn't just that I liked them: they made me feel happy."

You spoke in short sentences with long pauses between each word. You spoke like the protagonist of a slow and beautiful movie. I spoke like a comedy actor who'd gotten his first serious role and was trying to prove his versatility to the world, but only came off as pathetic because his effort was so obvious.

We went into the Mad Toy bookstore. I stopped by there every day and usually stayed for a long time, sometimes all afternoon, talking with one of the three owners, especially Miguel. I considered Miguel practically my best friend, but I also liked talking to Chino or Denise—they had all studied literature at the same university I went to now, and they weren't even thirty yet but they'd managed to open that tiny, excellent bookstore, which, in spite of its excellence or perhaps because of it, was headed straight off a cliff. They didn't sell bad books, or at least they tried not to. They arranged the shop-window and the displays according to a shared idea of literature on which they prided themselves. If someone asked for a book by an author they considered second-rate or commercial—which to them was exactly the same thing—Chino or Denise would go down to the storeroom to get it and would sell it grudgingly. But not Miguel. In those situations, Miguel would reply, opening his green eyes wide and almost unable to hide the satisfaction he felt at saying it, "We don't sell that kind of book here."

You and I looked at the Mad Toy's displays and shelves, and for thirty or forty minutes life consisted only of enthusiastically recommending books to each other, of rejoicing when our tastes coincided, and of constructing the tacit fiction that we would eventually read all those books together.

"I live really close to here," you told me suddenly. "I'd like to invite you over to watch a movie, but I have to go now. I need to walk my dog."

You paid for the book by Olga Orozco you'd been paging through and then you hurried off. For a brief moment, I surrendered to the fatalistic thought that I would never see you again.

"She comes in here a lot," Miguel told me then. "Usually around noon, or even earlier, at eleven or so. She spends a long time looking at books. Sometimes she buys two or three; other times she writes something down in a little red notebook and leaves without buying anything."

"What does she buy? Always poetry?"

"Poetry and essays. And philosophy. But novels, too, sometimes. Do you like her? Are you into her?"

I got nervous. I felt as though the question, in addition to being direct and sardonic, held a certain cruelty.

"She's different."

"Different from who?"

"I don't know. Everyone, I guess."

My friend laughed and I felt exposed, defenseless. I wanted to leave the bookstore, but Miguel, perhaps aware that I was uncomfortable, went out to buy coffee at Las Lanzas. I loved those rare minutes when I was left in charge of the store, as would theoretically happen in the future, if sales ever picked up—they wanted me to work there, but said there was no

way to afford it for now. We drank our coffee and I tried to
help Miguel, who was foundering in front of a Microsoft
Excel spreadsheet, and then I sat in a corner to look through
a few poetry anthologies. None of them had any poems by
Olga Orozco.

Toward the end of the afternoon, the TV actor Álvaro
Rudolphy strode in with all the confidence befitting his immense popularity. He flashed Miguel a TV-worthy smile before saying, all swagger, "Hey, buddy, recommend a book
for me."

"I can't. I don't know you," Miguel replied dryly and immediately. "How can I recommend a book for you if I don't
even know you?"

Rudolphy left the bookstore flustered and even humiliated,
and we were rolling with laughter as we closed the place up.

"Let's grab a bite at Dante," Miguel said.

"How can I grab a bite with you when I don't even know
you?" I replied.

We ate chacarero sandwiches and drank a few beers, drawing out the joy of that new phrase that worked for anything,
resolved everything. How can I split an order of fries with
you when I don't even know you? How can I pass the mus-
tard when I don't even know you? How can I pay if I don't
even know you? It wasn't that we didn't like Rudolphy, that
wasn't it at all—in fact, we thought he was quite a good actor. Still, the memory of his shocked face felt like an odd
kind of triumph.

Miguel went home, and I sat for almost an hour on a
bench in Plaza Ñuñoa in case you turned up, walking your
dog. It was hard for me to accept that I had to go home. I got

on the bus at almost midnight and dozed the whole way, my head bouncing against the window when I nodded off.

The next day I woke up to the infernal noise of the juicer. This was, unfortunately, a regular trick of my father's—he hated for the rest of the family to still be asleep by the time he'd finished reading the sports section, the only part of the paper that interested him. But he did have the courtesy to squeeze four extra oranges and leave a glass amid the piles of books on my bedside table.

"You can't be reading twenty or thirty books all at the same time, son," he told me.

I was going to reply that I could very easily be reading twenty or thirty books all at the same time, and that some of those books, like the poetry ones, I would never truly finish, but instead I pretended I was still asleep.

"You need to cut your hair," he told me then. "Before New York. People will discriminate against you if you go there with long hair."

He left the room, and for a few seconds I entertained the hope that he wouldn't come back. I sat up to chug the orange juice, then stared at the ceiling with the empty glass to my lips. My father had come back into my room and I could feel his expectant eyes on me, but I wouldn't meet them.

"Are you going to cut your hair? Yes or no?"

"No."

"If you don't cut your hair, you're not going to New York."

"Then I'm not going to New York. I don't care about New York. I'm not cutting my hair."

It was more or less true that I didn't care about New York. What did I know about New York back then? Whatever I'd gleaned from watching *Seinfeld* or *Taxi Driver*? Whatever I more or less understood from Frank Sinatra's hackneyed song? Any destination would have seemed equally awe inspiring to me, because although I'd backpacked around a good bit of Chile by bus and train, I had never set foot on an airplane.

The trip was a gift, and a completely unexpected one, because my father and I had been arguing over anything and everything for years. Nothing out of the ordinary—ours was the classic version of the father–son conflict, and I knew it, but knowing it didn't console me, didn't satisfy me, because my father always shouted louder and never apologized afterward. But after an especially turbulent fight he had found that way of saying sorry: he'd cashed in miles for a ticket in my name, trusting, and rightfully so, in the element of surprise, because he had chosen the date and that destination, which sounded so abstract and so spectacular.

"You're not going to New York, then, you blew it," my father said, incredulous. "You'll be on your knees, begging me. You're going to regret this."

"I won't regret it."

As I put my brand-new, sovereign decision into words, I felt dizzy from the weight of crucial, definitive sentences. And then I made another decision: I was going to move out of the house for good.

"Okay. The ticket's canceled," my dad told me a couple of hours later: he'd just gotten off the phone with the airline.

"Great," I said.

"So what time should we start the driving lesson?"

"No time, never."

"But we agreed."

"But now we're fighting."

"You know very well that those two things have nothing to do with each other."

"Yes, they do."

I spent the weekend locked in my room paging through those twenty or thirty books on my nightstand. Monday and Tuesday I looked for a new place to live. I had some savings from an assistantship and a summer job, but everything I looked at was outside my price range. I started to despair, because my only Plan B was to live at home and suppress my rage, but finally, almost miraculously, I found a cheap room in an apartment across from the National Stadium, very close to the university.

I would move in on Thursday, so I had one full, final day, which I spent inspecting every corner of my parents' house as if I were storing up material for future memories. Then I walked through my neighborhood trying to become a stereotypical social climber: I willed myself to look down my nose at the streets where I'd grown up, inventing a detachment, a contempt and resentment that in reality I didn't feel. I encouraged myself by imagining endless interesting conversations—I hadn't yet disowned the word *interesting*—with all my new friends, elbows propped on a table at Las Lanzas or Los Cisnes. Even the inhospitable lawns of the university campus struck me, suddenly, as an acceptable version of *locus amoenus*.

I talked to my mom and sister and asked them to keep my secret. They reacted with a mixture of trepidation and solidarity that for some reason I found disconcerting. When they went to bed, I stayed in the dining room and turned on the TV. There was no need for us to plan; it was understood that my father would come home right before the Colo-Colo game started. And that was what happened. We hadn't spoken to each other in days, but we watched the match together and even exchanged a few sentences, "That should be a red card!" or "He wasn't offsides," things like that. I don't remember who won. I think there were no goals, or else there were, and it was us, my dad and me, who were deadlocked.

My father raised his eyebrows to say "good night." I didn't go to bed. That night, I wrote the "Letter to My Father." Back then, I hadn't yet read Kafka's "Letter to His Father." I don't think I even knew it existed. I typed my version out on the household computer, since I didn't want my handwriting to ruin the message. I chose Century Gothic font in a very large size, maybe eighteen- or twenty-point, in case my father read the letter without his contacts in. He only ever took them out to sleep, but for some reason I imagined him holding the paper up to his naked eyes—his real ones, so to speak.

After everyone had left the next morning, I printed out the missive, all twelve pages. It wasn't an aggressive letter. It was melodramatic and tender, though I'd done my best to avoid tenderness. I wrote, maybe, as if I were the adult, and I had to explain that leaving home was the only way to keep

from hating him and from hating myself. I put it in an envelope, erased the file from the hard drive, and started packing
my books into trash bags. I caught myself counting them:
ninety-two. My friend Leo Pinos came over with a borrowed
truck, though a small car would have sufficed to transport
my ninety-two books and some clothes.

+ + + + +

"Everything I have to say is in the letter," I told my father,
with something like literary pride, when we saw each other
again the next Friday.

"I didn't read it."

"Seriously?"

"I'll read it next time I feel like crying. Except I never feel
like crying."

All I wanted to know was what he had thought or felt
when he'd read the letter; it had never occurred to me that he
would refuse to read it. We were in a minuscule conference
room at his office, as if laying out the strategic plan for a
small business. It was unclear what we had to talk about. Or
maybe it was clear, but there was just too much. My dad strung
together a very general speech that sounded like it was lifted
from a self-help book for fathers and sons. I focused on the
authority in his severe but deliberately softened voice. I noticed, as I often did, the burst blood vessels in his eyes, especially the left one: they were like tiny tributaries of a river
that seemed to indicate a kind of suffering whose origin
and terminus I couldn't presume to know. It was my father's

suffering, but also mine. The suffering of meeting my father's eyes and realizing that I didn't know him, that I had lived my whole life with someone I did not know and never would.

"So do we understand each other?"

I hadn't heard what he'd said, or I'd heard only the presumed music of his voice.

"I wasn't listening," I said.

"What?"

"I got distracted."

He came out with a few more words, badly faking a remnant of patience. I started to shout at him; I don't know what I said, but he just stared at me unfazed, like a politician or a dead man.

"Let's not overdo it," he interrupted me. "You're overreacting, you always do this. You left, it's done. Kids leave home much sooner in other countries. In the United States, you'd be considered a late bloomer. And I'm happy, because now I have another room in the house. I'm going to put a big TV in there so I can stay up until five in the morning watching movies."

I was late to Schuster's class again. I didn't feel like going, but I thought maybe I would run into you. You weren't there. Hardly anyone was, because the class was being taught by the T.A., who didn't smoke a single cigarette in the whole session. It was a different kind of class and really a very good one, full of ideas that seemed new. I remember we read some fragments of *The Cardboard House* by Martín Adán and a poem by Luis Omar Cáceres, the first lines of which were immediately seared into my memory, as if I'd known them forever: "Now that the road is dead / and our convertible reflection licks its ghost / with a dumbstruck tongue . . ."

Maybe I walked a few blocks to the rhythm of that poem, skipping Methodology again and heading straight to Plaza Ñuñoa. I wanted to talk to Miguel, though when I got to the Mad Toy I realized that what I really wanted was to talk to you. I asked Miguel if you'd been by the bookstore, and he said no.

"You're going to be okay," he told me after hearing my news.

He asked for details, lots of details. He asked if I needed anything, money, something else.

"What I need is work," I told him.

"Well, I can't give you a job," he said. "I almost don't have one myself. We're going to shut down, it's inevitable."

"When?"

"In a couple months, if we're lucky. We'll try to hold out until Christmas, but we won't make it past that."

"Shit, that's awful."

"So we can't hire you."

"Right, of course."

The fantasy of working at the Mad Toy had been a magical cure-all for me, but at that moment I wasn't thinking about my imminent lack of money. Instead, I was saddened by the thought of that place emptied out, surely taken over by some café or stupid hair salon. On a shelf I found *Defense of the Idol*, the only book Luis Omar Cáceres ever published, and I read every poem in it two or three times. Every once in a while Miguel said something and I answered him, and at times it was like the friendly, intermittent dialogue between two strangers sitting together by chance in a doctor's waiting room or at a wake. But when I was about to leave he handed me a sheet of paper on which he'd written down the phone numbers of ten people who might be able to give me a job of some kind: as a Latin tutor, a gofer, a house sitter, an assistant to an assistant editor.

"I'm going to let my hair grow out in solidarity with you," he told me as we hugged goodbye.

I bought some fresh-baked dobladitas and four slices of cheese and walked toward my new home thinking about the Mad Toy with anticipatory nostalgia. At the same time, I was also imagining another version of myself walking down some unknown New York avenue, sporting short hair and a dazed or amazed expression. I imagined myself as a young tree, a young and newly pruned tree that wanted to lengthen out and reach the sun's rays so it can grow some more. That's what I was thinking about when I sensed your presence, and there you were, almost stepping on my heels, with your dog.

"We've been following you for blocks. Chasing you."

I didn't believe you, but then I had the feeling that, yes, you had been close to me for a while.

"How come?"

"I wanted you to meet Flush."

Flush was a little black sausage-shaped mutt with damp eyes who moved pompously, seemingly removed from the world. At first I thought she was limping, but then I thought it was more that she embellished her steps with coy little hops. You talked to me about *Flush*, the Virginia Woolf book that your dog was named after, and you gave me a copy of *The Subterraneans*, a Jack Kerouac novella that I'd never heard of and that I read soon after, and still reread every two or three years, eager to experience, once again, the warm earthquake of that ending, one of the best I've ever read.

We reached my building and sat down halfway up the steps. I made cheese sandwiches, and the dog ate one, too. In just a week, everything had changed radically, and I tried to explain it all to you. But to do that I had to tell you my whole life story, which was not overflowing with events, though maybe just then I thought it was. I told you everything, or almost everything. I talked for some two hours, and it was getting dark when I ran out of words and waited for yours, which didn't come.

"Let's go inside. It's a little cold" was all you said.

The owner of the house was with some tourists—Canadians, I think—who were going to rent the other bedrooms; the owner and her daughters would sleep in the living room, in sleeping bags. She offered us some wine, but we went to my room instead. You stretched out on the mattress casually, as if you lived there. Flush lay at your feet and gnawed on her leash so you would take it off. I tried to straighten up the room a little; I hadn't had time to get a shelf for the books, and they were still in garbage bags, same as my clothes.

The light from a distant streetlamp shone dimly through the window. I watched you talk, barely moving your lips. You talked about your dead mother and the movies that she and your dad used to watch and that you now watched with him—"Gabriela loved this part," your dad would interject with an enthusiasm that for you was both moving and painful. And then you talked about insomnia and the medications you took for insomnia and a novel about insomnia that you wanted to write. And about a friend who had drowned years ago, in Pelluhue. And about four or five people you hated—high school classmates, I think, and an ex-boyfriend. I remember thinking that those people didn't deserve your hatred or anyone else's, but I didn't say so. I also remember feeling suddenly and intensely glad that you didn't hate me. At one point, out of nowhere, you burst out crying, and I tried to console you.

"It's just, your dad makes me so mad," you said.

"That's why you're crying? Because of my dad?" I asked.

"I don't know. I'm not crying for any reason, I'm not sad," you said. "I never cry over anything in particular. I'm just used to crying. I'm in favor of tears."

"Me, too," I said, smiling.

"I don't know why I cry. Sometimes I think I'm posing, all the time. I'm not like this."

"I like how you are. Even though I don't know what you're like. And I'm posing, too, all the time. With you and everyone else."

"Yeah."

Then came a long silence, an important and pleasant one. Like someone memorizing a shopping list, I thought back over the details of our conversation so I wouldn't forget a thing.

"Do you think your dad is ever going to read the letter?" you asked me then.

I had only just told you about that letter, and yet I felt as though that part of the conversation had been left definitively behind. It was hard for me to get my head back into the situation; it felt like that conversation with my dad was left far in the past, too. I tried to answer honestly. I thought my father had in fact already read the letter, but decided to tell me that he hadn't.

"Yeah, he read it, I'm sure of that," you said.

Flush was sprawled out and snoring. You went to the bathroom, and when you came back you flopped onto the bed again. Ten seconds later, as if you'd just remembered something urgent, you got back up, turned on the light, and started to take my books out of the bags one by one. Almost without looking at them, you piled them up like towers.

"This is your New York," you told me then. "See, these are the buildings in Manhattan, the skyscrapers."

We stacked the books into teetering, slapdash replicas of the Empire State Building, the Chrysler Building, and the Twin Towers, which were still standing then. We hadn't kissed yet, hadn't yet slept together, and we didn't know anything with any certainty about the future. Perhaps I intuited or fantasized that we would spend a long time together, several years, maybe our whole lives. But I had no idea that those years would be fun, intense, and bitter, and would be followed by a much longer, perhaps indefinite period during which we knew nothing of each other, until the moment came when it would seem possible, conceivable, to tell a story—any story, this story—and erase you from it. Just then you were utterly unerasable, then and for all time. And no thought about the future really mattered to us that night we spent using my books as the bricks in those buildings, imposing, distant, faraway, cold, absurd and beautiful buildings.

An Introduction
to Soccer Sadness

I.

It was, for us, the only kind of perceptible male sadness. We lived in a shitty world, but the only thing that really seemed to affect the men around us was an adverse outcome in Sunday's game. Just as the two or three hours after a win were opportune for asking them for permission or money, any time our fathers sank into soccer sadness, we knew it was better to let them deal with the defeat on their own. Pouty and wounded, on those nights fathers became even more distant than usual, and were prone to doing weird things, like gazing out the window at the empty street with expressions of stern impotence, or humming songs by Albert Hammond or Julio Iglesias while they shined their shoes frenetically, interminably. But there's no point judging them now. It's too easy. Besides, that romanticism has lived on in us. There's no denying that their sons still experience soccer sadness; it has changed shape, but it's still alive in us, maybe more alive than ever.

II.

There was a time, long ago, when I wasn't all that interested in watching soccer on TV or listening to it on the radio, though of course I liked to kick the ball around with the neighborhood kids, and I even enjoyed going to the stadium. I proudly waved my flag and sported my Colo-Colo cap, and I had fun watching the subs doing vigorous warm-ups, or the referees dancing their timid little steps, or Severino Vasconcelos's dashing hair blowing in the wind, or the heroic acrobatics of the coffee sellers circulating deftly through the crowd, giant thermoses hung around their necks. Whatever happened with the ball, however, was more or less the same to me. It was hard for me to grasp the correlation between the intense and messy pickup games we played in the street and the monotonous sport that was played at the stadium, especially because of the almost complete absence of goals. I have the impression that, in those days, I went to a whole lot of games that ended nil–nil.

In order to watch the game in relative peace, our fathers had no choice but to ply us with ice cream, soda, and candied peanuts. Taking us to the stadium was a mistake, a terrible idea, but it was also a wager, a short- or medium-term investment, because our dads knew that at some point we would get distracted from our distractions, and ultimately be captivated by soccer's endearing slowness.

In my case this happened quickly: at seven years old I was already a full-on, die-hard fan. A Colo-Colo fan, just like my dad. It would have been great if I had liked the rival team, or any other team at all. Now I can't think of a more efficient way to kill the father—a much more effective method than my predictable grunge rebellion or the lacerating political arguments that came later. I knew of some cases of dissident kids: somehow, mysteriously, citing reasons that were unserious and banal—the Universidad Católica team had a better jersey, for example—they managed a plot twist, and their cheated and bewildered fathers had no choice but to coexist with the enemy on a daily basis.

It's not at all clear that we ever *chose* our soccer teams for ourselves. For many of us, that part of our paternal inheritance was the only one we never questioned. And even during the worst of our father–son fights, the possibility of sublimating our problems and watching a game together granted us a reasonable amount of familial hope, a momentary truce that allowed us to at least maintain the illusion of belonging.

III.

My relationship with soccer is not literary, but my connection to literature does have, in a way, a soccer-istic origin. My greatest influences as a writer were not Marcel Proust's colossal novel or the enduring poems of César Vallejo or Emily Dickinson or Enrique Lihn, but rather the radio transmissions of Vladimiro Mimica, the commentator for Radio Minería. None of my reading was ever as influential as the elegant spoken prose of the famous "goal-singer." I even used to record the games and lie in bed to listen, to enjoy them in a purely musical sense. Thanks to his cheerful mediation, even the most tedious or anodyne games seemed like epic battles.

Vladimiro's voice was synonymous with soccer joy, but it could also happen, when I went back and listened to his play-by-plays of painful games, that I'd fall prey to the magical thinking that maybe the recording would not repeat reality. Maybe it would create a new one, not all that marvelous or different from the real one, maybe every bit as atrocious, but one where at least my team triumphed. Clearly, I was already suffering from chronic soccer sadness.

At home and of course at school I was forbidden to curse, but at the stadium I enjoyed the freedom to express myself with loud and clear profanity. There was a time when I would spend the whole game insulting the opponents and the refereeing trio. But cursing isn't as fun once it's officially allowed. Since we often went to doubleheaders (held due to the scarcity of stadiums) at the Santa Laura, I turned to announcing the first game at the top of my lungs—during the week, sitting in the classroom's back row, I studied the Chilean league sticker albums and tried to memorize all the teams' lineups, so I usually didn't make mistakes; except for one or two isolated complaints, no one seemed to mind my performance. My shift at that nonexistent radio station ended, however, when Colo-Colo came onto the field to play the main match. Then I became just another fan, apprehensive and testy, watching the game with clenched teeth, in a state of absolute tension.

IV.

Experts concur that the degree of soccer sadness a person experiences is inversely proportional to their expectations. Perhaps this sounds obvious. Okay, it *is* obvious, and it also doesn't seem like a theory that applies only to the "soccer blues," but I guess a little color never hurt anyone.

In the case of those of us who are fans of the so-called big teams, expectations are always too high: we demand that our team tear it up and thump the opponent week after week, so even a narrow victory after a badly played game can provoke a certain amount of soccer sadness. That triumphalism is grating: we're like those parents who, instead of congratulating and fawning over their children when they get a good grade, tell them only that they have done their duty. The situation of a fan, of a fanatic, becomes stifling; that's why we so enjoy games in which we don't identify at all with either team. We feel practically Buddhist in front of the TV, finally able to take a break from ourselves and truly enjoy the game.

I suspect that all big-team fans have at some point in their lives fantasized about switching teams. It's a reasonable, redemptive temptation to free ourselves from the pressing need to win all the time, in order to savor instead the partial, debatable small-team wins: staying in the first division; scoring a point or two on the big teams; losing, but with dignity, after leaving it all on the field; or else enduring decisive and humiliating losses, but only after dishing out a potpourri of brutal tongue-lashings to the much-better-paid stars of the opposing team. And there are those who took that voluntary step, which for most of us remained no more than a shameful flight of fancy, almost always impossible to confess. Once you get to a certain age—in my case, eight years old—changing teams is simply impossible.

V.

There was no need to switch to a smaller team, really: the Chilean national selection *was* our small team. Before Marcelo Bielsa and the "golden generation" spoiled us with dreams of a splendid future full of World Cup wins, the Chilean team had almost always been the one that was destined to fail, but that still, every once in a while, allowed us to flirt with glory from a decorous distance. "The Chilean team plays great / but just can't catch a break," Nicanor Parra wrote somewhere, and that was almost always how we felt. In any case, when Chile played, our broken and divided country seemed momentarily reconciled. In fact, we did suspend our differences; we enjoyed soccer collectively, though more than enjoyment it was about acknowledging a common suffering. For my generation, that suffering included the trauma of Cóndor Rojas and the deplorable episode when he faked an injury at the Maracanã, which FIFA quickly discovered and punished by banning Rojas for life and eliminating Chile from the qualifiers for the next World Cup. The concept of soccer sadness does not go far enough to describe what we felt in those years.

The small-team woes of the Chilean national selection were prodigiously offset by Colo-Colo's triumph at the 1991 Libertadores Cup. But when our thoughts returned to our small, blackballed national team, the depression returned. In the midnineties, we dealt with our World Cup ostracism by cheering on Iván Zamorano's triumphs in Spain. There was a perversion there—suddenly, for us, soccer was no longer a team sport: the whole of Chile stopped what it was doing to watch Real Madrid's games, and if Zamorano scored a goal it brought the house down. And if he was substituted—for us, always unfairly—we didn't give a rat's ass about the fate of Real Madrid, though we stuck close to the TV just to jinx those strikers who were trying to take his place.

VI.

I interrupt this essay to come clean about a shameful episode, one that invalidates me as a fan and perhaps also as a person: for almost two years, I pretended not to like soccer.

My only excuse, valid but inadequate, is youth. Nor can love work as a mitigating factor, though it all started in the midst of courtship: things were going well, Anastasia and I had been walking aimlessly for hours, though that was only a delay tactic. We both knew the evening would end in the first kisses and caresses we were so eager for, which would play out in the semidarkness of some peaceful plaza finally emptied of nosy kids and those ubiquitous retirees who employ the cheap trick of feeding pigeons in order to indulge their wanton voyeurism.

"Hey, you don't like soccer, right?"

That's what Anastasia asked me. There was a sort of implicit plea in her voice, or at least I thought so.

"Of course not."

I lied instinctively, but also out of habit. Anastasia, on the other hand, never lied. She was extremely honest, perhaps overly so, as I later found out definitively but began to see that very night, when she told me all about her previous boyfriend. He was a sensational guy, her soulmate, they both knew every Cure song by heart, even the ones they didn't like, because really they liked them all. And they could also both recite long passages from Ernesto Sábato's *On Heroes and Tombs*; they'd even taken a trip to Buenos Aires in order to experience, to re-create, to recover, to *live* that novel. But Anastasia had never been able to accept her boyfriend's interest—excessive, in her opinion—in soccer. At first she'd thought that his exaggerated passion was a minor, reversible defect, but soon it had become clear that her boyfriend was a lost cause: every other week he'd stand her up to go to the stadium, and on a daily basis he used those soccer metaphors that she found so irritating ("Let's get a game plan," he'd say, for example, whenever they were deciding what to do). Her boyfriend's passion for soccer was not the official or the main reason for the end of that relationship, but it had played a role.

"Personally, I've always thought soccer was pretty dumb," I told her, with persuasive cynicism. "It's just nine dumbasses running around after a ball."

"Aren't there eleven? Eleven per team, so twenty-two?"

"To be honest, I have no idea," I went on, inspired. "I'm a philistine when it comes to soccer, I've never even watched a show."

"You mean a match."

"Right, a match."

She looked at me as though I'd just said something amazing, and then she launched into an extraordinary and seemingly endless tirade against soccer. Her words hurt me, partly because, stuck as I was in the character I'd just created, I couldn't object, and also because my neck started to ache from all the nodding. I tried to distract myself by looking at her hair, freshly dyed a color halfway between red and orange, or her teeth, which were almost unrealistically white and small, and also very odd, because they seemed to have been arranged in pairs, with notable gaps between one pair and another, as if she had taken them out and rearranged them in a moment of boredom.

Anastasia talked about sexism, nationalism, and barbarity, and her arguments all struck me as affective (back then I believed, as so many PhDs and national senators still think, that the word *affective* meant *efficient* or *effective*). Her position summarized the opinions of nearly all of my professors and classmates regarding soccer, especially since violence in stadiums had become a subject of national debate. Even I, after I'd been spat on by a fan from the rival team and mugged by a hooligan from my own, had stopped going to the stadium.

Maybe during that time I also had an anti-soccer impulse that was linked to my social climbing impulse and my desire to belong to that community of skeptical, critical, bullshitting intellectuals who held soccer in such contempt. It was similar to my attitude toward music throughout my adolescence, in a time that wasn't as propitious for the eclecticism that's so prized now: I had started out liking folk music and then moved on to thrash metal, then New Wave, punk, and then back to folk, with all the ensuing changes in dress, friends, and even habits.

VII.

Soon, Anastasia and I got lost in conversations about Krzysztof Kieślowski's *The Double Life of Veronique* and the *Three Colors* trilogy, and we also assembled, with the urgent speed of intense love, a soundtrack that even included a few—certainly not all—Cure songs, as well as a broad range of literary concurrences that only excluded, for obvious reasons, *On Heroes and Tombs*. (I think I managed to convince her that *Abaddón, the Exterminator* was better, though I was never really sure that it was; honestly, even today I couldn't definitively say whether I like any of Ernesto Sábato's books, except for *The Tunnel*, which is probably his least good, but I'm in no position to say, since, like every Chilean kid who was into books, I went crazy for it when I was around twelve years old, so that it possesses, for me, the indisputable status of a personal classic.)

I don't want to caricature my relationship with Anastasia. Well, not too much, anyway; sometimes it's inevitable and even advisable to caricature, since it allows us to forgive those other people we once were. Though in reality the ones we should forgive are the insensitive grown-ups we are today, capable of minimizing something that was—and we know this, but pretend not to—enormous and serious and wonderful. We talk about the past and laugh at ourselves as if our future selves were never going to laugh at who we are now. Sorry, I don't want to run on here: I was trying to say that Anastasia and I very quickly built a relationship of absolute companionship and dizzying trust, and even so, I never owned up to my cowardly parallel romance with soccer.

VIII.

By the time the Chilean national selection returned to the international arena to compete in the 1998 French World Cup qualifiers (which at the time, maybe to induce a very reasonable pessimism, we called *knockouts*), Anastasia and I were practically living together. I had to make up one excuse after another in order to watch the games hidden away in some bar or ensconced on the cold sofa at my parents' house. But sometimes I just couldn't escape, and it was hard to overcome the bitterness I felt as I strolled through a deserted park with Anastasia, or maybe watched some weighty and profound

Fellini film, right at the moment when all of Chile was cheering for our team.

I can pinpoint my worst memory in this regard precisely on the evening of November 16, 1997: seventy thousand fevered souls packed the National Stadium, thrilled about Chile's likely qualification for the World Cup in France, while Anastasia and I, a few blocks away, protected by the half darkness of the closed blinds, were trying to screw.

"What's going on out there?" I asked in medias res, when the crowd exploded with joy over the opening goal.

"I think there's a match," Anastasia told me. "Chile's playing—the national team, la Roja."

"Julián Zamorano must've scored," I said.

"*Iván* Zamorano," Anastasia corrected me.

"Right, that's the one, Iván."

My ruse was twofold, since I knew perfectly well that Zamorano was injured. So, while the Chilean players gave it their all out on the pitch, we were inside listening to *OK Computer* on my auto-reverse stereo. Sometimes, when I listen to that album now, I catch myself trying uselessly to remember or guess which Radiohead song was playing in my room when Chamuca Barrera took off on that miraculous run that culminated in an exquisite goal, or when, a few minutes later, with his usual clinical finishing, Matador Salas started paving the way to victory, or when, toward the end of the game, Candonga Carreño headed the winning goal, ensuring our presence in the 1998 World Cup after sixteen years away.

IX.

A new soccer concept that my son has recently invented is the *self-foul*, coined spontaneously one day when he tried to kick the ball and fell over on his own. That's exactly what my whole relationship with Anastasia was: the regrettable and prolonged result of an absurd self-foul.

I'll finish the story real quick. While I was in the shower one morning, Anastasia went through my clothes and found my Colo-Colo jersey. I should have gotten mad and asked her why she was riffling through my stuff, but I felt like I'd been caught red-handed. I explained that it had been a birthday present from my dad, and that in spite of our turbulent relationship, the shirt had sentimental value. She remembered the Católica jersey her ex-boyfriend had given her and we turned it into a joke. I should have seen that incident as a warning or a portent of what was to come.

"You know very well why," Anastasia told me a few weeks later when she broke up with me.

I've noticed that, these days, instead of saying "terminó conmigo" (she ended it with me), people are saying "me terminó," or "she ended me." I think this new formula is great, because that's exactly what I felt then: she ended me, liquidated me, annihilated me. She took out my batteries, unplugged me, cut my cables, and stored me in a box in the attic forever. Later, thanks to the indiscretion of our mutual friends, I found out that my constant absences and excuses had made her conclude that I had a lover, or several. I never cheated on her, but it was still hard for me to argue, because in actual fact I was leading a double life. I was disconsolate, especially when I found out from the same bigmouthed friends that she had a new boyfriend just two weeks after our breakup. I spent months insisting that we get together, because I wanted to at least clarify things. It was hard to convince her to see me.

"My boyfriend is upstairs in my room," she told me, I guess in order to humiliate me, the day we finally did meet up.

"I just want you to know the truth," I said, and maybe I even imagined a drumroll before I came out with the next words, which must have sounded perfectly idiotic. "The thing is, I like soccer. I like soccer a lot. I've always liked it. Sometimes I even dream I'm scoring goals in stadiums full of people. Magnificent goals. Acrobatic and unforgettable ones. And that's the whole truth."

She looked at me in shock, the contempt frozen on her face. I went on talking about how much I liked soccer, and I assured her that all those times she'd thought I was cheating on her, I was actually watching a game, with friends or with my dad.

"With your dad? I thought you hadn't spoken to him in years!"

"That's just what I told you, to throw you off. The truth is we don't talk much. We watch soccer and talk about it, that's all."

"That's the most unbelievable excuse you could have possibly come up with. Don't you supposedly want to be a writer?"

"But . . ."

Just then, the boyfriend appeared in the living room and put an end to the visit. I saw him again many times after that; I ran into him almost every week at the vegetable stand full of rotten tomatoes and rancid lettuce where we both bought our weed. I said hi to him, of course—I always say hi—and he also greeted me, raising his eyebrows with a kind of cheerful indifference. Later I found out he was a fan of Universidad de Chile, but every time I saw him he was wearing the shirt of a different soccer team: Real Madrid, AC Milan, Manchester United, Inter de Porto Alegre, San Lorenzo de Almagro. He was one of those global fans who were starting to emerge in those days, and that now you can always find frequenting wine stores, bike races, music festivals, and record shops. I have to admit that every one of those jerseys looked good on him.

I learned my lesson, or maybe my stupidity just changed shape over the years. Later I was lucky enough that soccer stopped being, for me, a purely masculine endeavor. I didn't deserve it, but fate rewarded me with two female friends who were soccer fans and Colo-Colo addicts, thanks to whom I realized that the passion for soccer is not at all exclusive to men. I went back to the stadium with them, first in the extraordinary years of the Colo-Colo four-time league championships under Claudio Borghi, and later to see the illustrious national team of Bielsa and the golden generation of Arturo Vidal, Alexis Sánchez, Claudio Bravo, Mauricio Isla, et al.

Later I started to spend more time away from Chile, and although soccer never lost importance for me, it did become an almost purely televised and solitary experience. I even adopted the habit of watching matches while riding a stationary bike, as though playing a kind of analog Wii. Sometimes I still do it: if Pibe Solari is running down the wing, I pedal faster, and if Colorado Gil or Vicente Pizarro is trying to run out the clock, I slow down.

X.

Of all available TV programs, soccer is the only one not governed by the imperatives of information or entertainment. Commentators and pundits can spend the full ninety minutes talking about how bad the game is, and it never even occurs to them that they could lose their viewers, because in fact that possibility does not exist. Those who watch the game are a loyal, captive audience, and we'll stay right there, hypnotized, or in the worst case lulled to sleep by the lack of action. And not even our own snores, or the suspicion that the game remained every bit as boring during the minutes we were dozing, will make us change the channel or turn off the TV.

There's a certain beauty in these scenes of honest, sober boredom. But TV broadcasts are always a little redundant anyway. Radio commentators are poets who leap from metaphor to metaphor with admirable speed, or else they're skilled classical storytellers with recognizable and even study-able styles, able to *make the unknown known* just through a couple of brushstrokes. TV commentators, meanwhile, are condemned to repeat what we're watching with our own two eyes, telling a story we already know. It's a difficult profession, though perhaps the hardest job is that of the pundits, with whom we rarely agree. Except when they are retired players whom we've loved and respected in the past, pundits receive our invariable, perhaps excessive and unfair, contempt.

I felt that way especially about the sports journalist Felipe Bianchi: I always disagreed with his game analysis, and even when I agreed I invented some nuance to nitpick. Later, through a series of random coincidences, I had the privilege of getting to know him, and well: he turned out to be a very nice guy, compassionate, generous, and sometimes surprisingly shy. Sooner rather than later we became friends, so that when I saw him on TV reviewing a game or starting debates on the news, I tried to recite that list of virtues, but it was no good: I still couldn't stand him. And that was in the years of Bielsa and Sampaoli, when the national team almost always won.

All of this is background to get to the moment when, thanks to another series of flukes, Felipe and I were both living in New York, and we would get together to watch Chile play in the Centennial Copa America. Nothing better than to watch the game with a dear friend, both of us on pins and needles. We'd have a drink, snack on a cheese plate, turn on the TV, all as it should be, but from time to time Felipe came out with some comment that was of course pertinent and intelligent and yet I couldn't help but contradict him, and sometimes I outright shushed him. At the risk of being impolite, it was very hard for me to squander that chance to shush the TV pundit, even if he was no longer just a pundit but also a faithful friend who showed up with Belgian beer and rare, excellent cigarettes. In spite of his famous ferocity and his well-earned reputation as a polemicist, Felipe, oddly, accepted my disapproval or my bad manners. Maybe he recognized in me the same impulse that had led him to become a pundit in the first place: the urge to silence the pundits.

XI.

My arrival in Mexico more or less coincided with Matías Fernández's arrival to Necaxa, which I took as an eloquent sign of benevolence from Our Lord Jesus Christ. During the year and a half that Mati played here, I followed his respectable performance as faithfully as ever, and when he left I really did try to keep supporting Necaxa, but soon had to accept that I was watching the games without much interest, or with the average interest I feel watching any match of any league from any random country in the world.

The Mexican league is superior to the Chilean one in almost every sense, but once you get to a certain age—in my case, exactly forty-two—it's impossible to get excited about any soccer but your own. Soccer is more idiosyncratic than we give it credit for. If there's a game on between the Pumas and the Chivas de Guadalajara, I'll watch it and even enjoy it in a calm, Zen-like way, but if at the same time, say, Ñublense are playing Antofagasta, I won't hesitate to tune into the Chilean league instead. Maybe it's just comforting to know that what I'm watching on the computer screen is happening in Chile. Or maybe deep down I still want to memorize the lineups of all the teams in the Chilean league. Maybe someday, if my son takes an interest in the sport, I'll finally thrill to Mexican soccer. But I don't know if I want my son to like soccer.

XII.

During my son's first two years of life I missed a lot of my team's games, nearly all of them. The part of me that wanted nothing more than to turn on the TV and watch soccer with my baby in my arms always lost by a landslide to the part of me that changed his diapers or sang lullabies or took him for walks in the stroller through Parque España. A little over a year ago, though, Colo-Colo's terrible season had them on the ropes, and I negotiated parenting shifts far in advance so I could witness it in real time as my team either maintained their dignity or went to shit. There was a chance Colo-Colo would no longer be a "big team," and the fans were suffering as never before in the institution's glorious history.

After one of those horrible games, my son peered up at me, intrigued by how absent or distracted I seemed.

"I'm sad, because Colo-Colo lost and they might get relegated to the second division," I explained.

Those words, more or less incomprehensible to him, stuck with him anyway. He's started regularly telling me—in the same exaggeratedly sweet tone I use when I console him—not to worry, that everything will be all right, that very soon Colo-Colo will start winning again, with goals scored by John Lennon, Frida Kahlo, and Batman and Robin Hood. (I haven't wanted to clear up his confusion there; maybe the world would be less unfair if instead of that good-for-nothing Robin, Batman's sidekick was Robin Hood.)

Just as my literary vocation is related to soccer, my son's halting soccer education had, in a way, a literary origin. One morning it occurred to me to have him listen to Mauricio Redolés's album *Bailables de Cueto Road*, which features the narration of an invented soccer match between Chile's living poets and its dead ones. The dead poets win 8–2, thanks to an excellent performance from the newly deceased Jorge Teillier, making his debut. Listening to Redolés, I was able to recover my passion for commentating by narrating other, equally unreal games for my son: Sea Animals versus Land Animals, Dinosaurs versus Non-Dinosaurs, The Beatles versus

Los Bunkers, Fingers versus Trees and Flowers, Months of the Year versus Chilean Volcanos, and so on.

Up to then my son had considered the ball to be just another toy—one with a curiously round shape, but a toy nonetheless—and he insisted on keeping it in the basket of stuffed animals; those commentaries, though, started him down the path. And thus began some very strange pickup games on our patio, because for my son the real game consisted of saying and making me say words like *crossbar*, *screamer*, *panenka*, or *toe poke*, or conjugating new verbs like *shimmy*, *dribble*, and *volley*, employing formulas like *yours*, *mine*, *to you*, *to me* (classic stock phrases of good old Vladimiro Mimica), or chanting *ball in the net ball in the net, dead, dead, dead* (courtesy of Ernesto Díaz Correa's unflagging throat), or *don't say goal, say golazo* (a pan-Hispanic clincher that in our version becomes eternal, because *golazo* turns into *golazazo* and *golazazazo* and so on).

The only time we've ever watched a game—a particularly bad one, the final of the 2021 European Championship between Italy and England—my son started out excited, jumping on the bed and cheering all the players' movements with bursts of his newly acquired verbal exuberance. But after about fifteen minutes, he went quiet and whispered into my ear in the beautiful tone of a secret, the way he does when he wants to emphasize that he is speaking seriously:

"Dad, I don't really understand soccer that much. What's happening?"

It was a boring game, that's all, I explained. I didn't want to tell him that the vast majority of games are every bit as boring as that one.

XIII.

"Why'd you name her Anastasia?" my wife asks.

It takes me a few seconds to realize she thinks Anastasia wasn't real, that I'm making her up.

"Because that was her name."

"Really? Like the Russian princess?"

"Right," I tell her.

"I thought she was a metaphor."

"For what?"

"For me."

She says she likes my story. I tell her it's an essay. She says she likes my essay, in a tone that makes it clear she thinks it's a story and she doesn't much like it. I ask her what it is she doesn't like. She tells me she likes everything except the soccer part. She says there are some jokes that she likes a lot and others she doesn't get, but she gets that they *are* jokes. She advises me to lie and say I've become a fan of women's soccer. I tell her it wouldn't be a lie, because in fact I followed the entire campaign of Chile's women's team in the 2019 World Cup in France.

"Name five players."

"Christiane Endler, Carla Guerrero, Javiera Toro, Francisca Lara, María José Rojas. That's five. Yessenia López, six. Rosario Balmaceda, seven . . ."

She thinks I'm making those names up. I tell her all about the harrowing elimination, Francisca Lara's penalty against the crossbar that could have been the 3–0 that would have gotten them into the last sixteen.

We get into the car, my wife at the wheel, thoughtful, while I ride in the back with our son. Often, of late, he's been getting mad when he feels left out of a conversation ("Don't talk to each other!" he implores us), but now he is listening attentively, as if trying to understand our debate from a philosophical point of view. But maybe he's not listening. Really, he is looking out at the trees, and maybe that's what he is trying to understand or decipher or absorb: the colorful enigma of jacaranda trees that move their branches in the breeze as though waving or begging for mercy. Or the atmosphere of the street corner, with its generous jugglers and unapproachable window washers, where we patiently wait out a long red light.

"You should talk about women's soccer, but you should especially talk about the violence of men's soccer, and the economic interests of corporations, and the absurd, macho competitiveness. You can get all that in if you develop Estefanía's arguments more."

"Anastasia," I note.

"But Estefanía is a prettier name."

"But her name was Anastasia."

"Well, make Anastasia more consistent. I don't really believe her as a character. Make her more serious."

"But that's how she was. And she does seem serious, I think."

"Make her more serious."

"But my story isn't that serious."

"Your essay."

My essay isn't serious.

Or maybe it is, I start to think: it's very serious.

Sadness is a very serious subject.

Aside from one uncle, a soccer hipster who likes to go

around the city in his Barcelona jersey, everyone in my wife's family, including her, claim to be fans of the Pumas from UNAM, the university they all went to. But I think my son has caught on that they are phony fans. Soccer isn't important or even interesting to them. As for my wife, she had a rough morning on the playground as a kid when she was hit in the face by three consecutive balls. Since then, she has associated soccer solely with the possibility of getting hit, and as such she stays cautiously on the sidelines of our pickup games.

"Have you finished your essay?" she asks me later that night as she tries to play a Belle & Sebastian song on our son's little red guitar.

"I'm missing the end, but I'm not going to write it yet."

"Why not?"

"I'll write it in a couple of weeks, once we know whether Chile is going to the World Cup in Qatar."

"Hopefully they don't go, Qatar is a massacre, it's one of the most unequal countries in the world. Is Mexico going?"

"Mexico always goes," I tell her. "It's easy for them, the Concacaf qualifiers are—"

"But Chile beat us seven–nil!"

"Yeah, but that was like five years ago. Everything is different now," I tell her ruefully.

XIV.

I'm writing these final lines on my phone while my son is at soccer class. The class was his mom's idea—she says she doesn't want him to go through life in constant fear of stray soccer balls. In today's class there are five girls and three boys, including my son. It's the first time they've been allowed to play without masks, so I'm finally seeing their faces and their big smiles, though at times they look endearingly concentrated on the instructions of a sweet, energetic coach, a woman in an official Pumas jersey. The class follows a system of gradual assimilation, so for now it seems like a class in anything but soccer: they play ring-around-the-rosy and tag, they jump in and out of hoops, they run around without order or coherence while waving ribbons. There are a couple of goals, but they're only used for taking shelter from an imaginary storm (when the rain is real, of course, class is canceled). There are also soccer balls—the field is covered with lightweight, colorful balls, which the kids happily kick any which way.

While I watch them run and jump, oblivious to any idea of competition, I think about when I used to attend the Cobresal Soccer School, Maipú branch, where I distinguished myself as one of the subs with the least chance of ever starting a game. I guess the coaches tried not to destroy our dreams too early on, but there was no way they would give me more than two or three minutes, always at the end of the game. That's why to this day I identify with the players who come on during injury time, just to run out the clock. I used to go home devastated, ruminating on the defeat in silence—not the team's defeat, but mine alone, and I always told my parents that I'd done well, that I was sure I'd get to start any day now.

But that was a different kind of soccer sadness, of course, and it will have to wait for another essay or story. As for our fathers' soccer sadness, so different but at times so similar to the soccer sadness felt by those of us who are now fathers, and as such attend the constant re-creation of our own childhoods—as for that sadness, after rereading these pages,

I have to admit that I have been terribly unfair. What our fathers felt when they saw their beloved teams win was not exactly joy, but a kind of slightly attenuated sadness. What I mean is: our fathers were sad, of course they were, every minute of every hour of all the days of their lives they were sad, and victory was only a respite, a palliative, a freebie, a token; it was a measly reprieve that let them temporarily believe that everything wasn't really so terrible. Plus, their soccer sadness humanized them, proved that they were fallible and childish, just like we were back then, like we are now. I think that's what Professor D. Zíper was getting at with this beautiful theory: "If soccer is the problem, childhood is the solution."

Oh, right: last night the Chilean team failed to qualify for the World Cup. Everyone saw it, everyone knows. I'm not going to talk about that now. I never want to talk about soccer again.

Blue-Eyed Muggers

I.

Once, I defended my father. Physically. It was a summer morning, and a mugger was about to kick him while he was down.

"That was in 1990, right?"

"Are you writing about me? Again? Enough is enough!" says my father.

For some months now, my dad has been calling my son every Saturday and Sunday morning. He has, quite unexpectedly, become an attentive long-distance grandfather: him in Chile, us in Mexico, separated by too many miles and almost two years of pandemic.

Silvestre waits for those calls. He always wakes up between six and six thirty and comes running into my room, which is actually his, because at some point during the night he woke up and moved to our bed—which as far as he's concerned is his mother's and his—and I moved to his bed, which is also, as such, a little bit mine.

"Dad, has Grandpa called yet?" he asks me eagerly.

I yawn and pick up my phone, and there is nearly always a message from my father that says "I'm ready." My father gets up early, he has gotten up early his whole life. I belong to the category of fathers who always want to snooze just another ten minutes. My dad belongs and has always belonged to the category of early-bird fathers. Plus, he's in the future, because of the time difference: three hours ahead. And maybe it's a good thing for fathers to live three hours in the future.

I open the curtains to let the daylight in, but the sun isn't up yet. Silvestre stacks his books and climbs on top of them to reach the light switch, all the while chatting enthusiastically with his grandfather. They devise plans, immediate and urgent ones; it's going to be a long and intense call, it always is—they'll talk for at least an hour.

From Monday to Friday we try to get Silvestre to dress himself, or at least we promote the fiction that he dresses himself. On weekends, however, as if we were seconds away from going on air, I dress him quickly myself and we go straight down to the living room, where I balance the phone against the wall, trying for a wide shot, like a security camera's. I make coffee and try to get breakfast going while they talk, but sometimes the phone falls over or my son moves out of frame.

"Alejandro, please, I can't see him!" my father complains instantly, like a diner who finds a hair in his soup.

Really, his tone harbors the same authority as always, but with a friendly shading: I suppose he knows I'm busy slicing a papaya or keeping an eye on the quesadillas. I go over to restore the communication, proceeding with efficient know-how, a little like a roadie midconcert. Sometimes I take advantage of that break to talk to him a little, to tell him something.

"I'm not writing about you, Dad," I lie.

"Why don't you write about the kid instead? He's a lot more interesting than me," he says, accurately.

"Well, I was thinking about that time we were assaulted. That was 1990, right?"

"Right."

I don't use the informal *tú* with my father, I never have. My sister does. For many years, I was oblivious to that difference. But there's an explanation for it. In my father's family everyone uses *tú* with each other, and my sister inherited that habit. I was closer to my mother's side and maybe that's why I picked up her custom of using the formal *usted*. Sometimes, using the formal tense with my father or mother seems warmer to me. But it's not. It's colder, it marks a distance. A distance that exists. A distance that every once in a while disappears and reappears without warning.

"You're going to write about that assault? A whole novel?"

"No, I couldn't get a whole novel out of that."

"Make it a novel, embellish it a little. Is it my biography?"

"No."

"I'm going to write your biography too, just you wait," he says. "I'll tell the whole truth then."

"And what will you call that book?"

"*Ways of Losing a Son.*"

II.

The story from 1990 is a simple one, and perhaps its only peculiarity is that I've never been able to tell it. That is, I've told it a thousand times, but only to friends, in the midst of those long gatherings that now I miss so much, when everyone took chaotic turns regaling the group with old anecdotes. It's an after-dinner story, one that perhaps requires the characteristic cheerful, good-humored tone in which unimportant tales are told.

I was fifteen, and my father was . . .

I get out the calculator, let's see: my father was born in 1948, so that morning in 1990 he must have been . . . 1990 - 1948 = 42 years old. No, 41, because it was February, and he was born in August.

My father, at forty-one, would have considered it humiliating to need a calculator for such a simple operation. Even today, at seventy-three, he would come up with the answer without hesitation, in less than a second. He wouldn't give the impression of having solved a math problem at all.

Then I was fifteen—no, fourteen, because it was in February and I was born in September. Back then, at fourteen years old, that summer of 1990, I would have done the math in my head, too.

The guy was about to kick my dad while he was down, but I stepped in and defended him. I kicked the blue-eyed mugger in the balls.

That's the story, in essence. I want to tell it slowly, like someone reviewing a questionable play frame by frame. Like someone figuring out whether or not the ball hit the defender's hand. Like someone looking for a continuity error.

The times I tried to write this story before, I did it in the third person. I almost always try in first and third person. And also in second, like my favorite novel, *A Man Asleep*, by Georges Perec. Then I choose the voice that sounds most natural, which is almost never the second person. There's something about this particular story, though, that made me try it only in third. Maybe because lately I've been reconciling with the third person. Because everything that happens, happens to everyone. Unequally, but to everyone. And in spite of the asymmetries, in spite of those differences, every once in a while I get the feeling that everything that happens to me also happens in the third person.

III.

During those calls my father and I speak little, sometimes not at all. They are the ones who talk, my father and my son. If I interject, my son will excitedly include me in the game, but if he gets the sense that my intention is, so to speak, informative—if I want to talk to my dad, in passing, about something serious—he can get mad.

My father and my son plan trips to Mars or to Chile, which for now are equally unlikely. They mix Spanish with an invented language that sounds like a kind of Russian with a German accent. Other times the game consists of improvising something that they call "a meeting." Their conversations are fast, confused, funny, delirious. At times my father's deep and lurching Chilean loses ground to my son's pristine Mexican. But they understand each other, always. My son gathers together a bunch of stuffed animals and my father does too, because over these years he has mitigated the distance by buying stuffed animals to give his grandson once they can finally see each other in person. My father becomes the supervisor of a small crowd of stuffed bears that look like dogs and dogs that look like bears. My son behaves like the charismatic leader of a squadron of space vagabonds.

"You want to say hi to your grandma?"

"Yeah."

This only happens sometimes. Only on occasion does my mother participate in these calls. And only for a few minutes, no more. My mother addresses my son with tender, ill-timed words. He listens to her with wavering curiosity. Hearing my mother's voice, seeing her face out of the corner of my eye, moves me, though she only spends a moment in the lime-light, her role is a mere cameo, because she wants to talk, not play, and this call is all about playing. She gets mad—pretend-mad, I assume—when she hears my son and my father inventing the dishes served up at Restaurant Gross: vomit puree, poop soup, pee lemonade, among other options that my son applauds effusively.

"Horacio, please, stop it," my mother tells my father.

Sometimes my son disengages from the call. He starts to draw, for example, while his grandfather talks to him. He doesn't leave the game, drawing is part of the game, and maybe ignoring his grandfather is too. Even as my father grows tired of insisting, my son knows the call isn't over. I like that absurd and beautiful form of companionship, that silence filled with activity. In recent weeks, ever since I decided to write this story, those are the moments I've used to ask my father about certain details, or even read him a few paragraphs. He listens to me with a mixture of impatience and genuine interest.

IV.

When I was fourteen years old, my father was still taller than me. As I understand it, people reach their definitive height at around twenty years old. In any case, I was a skinny, stooped, delicate kid who certainly didn't look capable of defending a stocky, brawny, athletic father with enormous hands. A goalie's hands.

My father's hands were and still are those of a man who has worked with his hands. At seven, nine, twelve years old, my father sold fruits and vegetables at the market in Renca. His hands also served to catch crosses and save penalties. My father's entire body has been, in general, useful. And it would have been much more so if not for the fact that his eyes went bad at a young age and were untreated for far too long.

He wanted to do military service, he wanted to become a policeman, he almost became the third goalie on the Colo-Colo youth team, but none of that worked out, partly because of his sick eyes. In all the photos of him as a young man, he's wearing some Coke-bottle glasses that make his face look a little like a mask. I inherited a manageable myopia, reasonable and even operable, though I never seriously considered surgery (the mere thought of lasers on my eyes is terrifying). At fourteen, I had already been prescribed glasses, but I never wore them; I still hadn't reached the age where leaving the house without glasses would be madness. An age I reached a while ago now. Even so, with all my myopia and astigmatism and the disturbing recent incursion of near-sightedness, my eyesight is still better than my father's was at forty-one years old.

When it's said that someone works with their hands, no one thinks about writers. Rightly so. We have the hands of exceptionally mediocre pianists. My father is not a writer, he never has been, never wanted to be. He was never interested in poetry. Though I do remember a day when he wrote a poem.

"It can't be that hard, Chile is a nation of poets," he said.

I don't remember the chain of events or words that led up to that brilliant statement. Then he grabbed a napkin and the pen he only used for signing checks, and without hesitation he wrote a poem that he read aloud to us immediately. We applauded. We were his captive audience. A generous, indulgent audience.

V.

So, that morning in 1990, we went downtown alone, my father and I. In the car, a Peugeot 504. We would be leaving that afternoon for a vacation in La Serena, and my father needed cash, more than he could take out from an ATM.

"Why did you need so much cash?"

"Because workers were going to paint the house while we were on vacation."

"And how come we went to the Santander downtown?"

"Santiago. Back then Santander was still called Banco Santiago."

"Why did we go to the Santander downtown and not to the Maipú branch?"

"I wanted to go downtown, I wanted to buy something at one of those stores on Bulnes. A fishing rod, something like that."

"But you worked downtown—why didn't you buy the fishing rod or take out money before the day we were leaving?"

"I don't remember! Maybe I wanted us to go downtown together. It was the first day of vacation, but I still wanted to go with you. I liked to take you downtown."

Ours, then, was an unnecessary trip. My dad parked where

he always does, on Agustinas and San Martín, near his office. We went straight to the bank, the branch on Bombero Ossa. While he waited in line, I sat reading in a corner. Suddenly, I felt watched or inspected or threatened, and I looked up and caught a glimpse of a young man's blue eyes. A second later the man was gone. My dad walked toward me, calmly and innocently counting the bills he had just received. I don't know how much money it was.

"Four hundred thousand pesos," he says, with certainty.

"And how much is that, in today's money?"

"I have no idea. Figure it out online!"

I figure it out online, and it takes a long time: one thousand three hundred dollars, more or less. In five-thousand-peso bills, that I remember.

"Why in fives? There were already tens in circulation by 1990."

"Really? Well, I don't know, maybe they weren't that common. Maybe they were too big, hard to change. The painters needed to buy materials."

I didn't think the blue-eyed man was dangerous. I didn't believe in the existence of blue-eyed muggers. But I still warned my dad that something strange was happening. And I was annoyed that he was so unconcerned, that he would count the bills right out in the open like that. He handed half the money to me, just in case. He smiled at me first, as though approving of my caution, my good judgment. Sometimes, when parents congratulate their children, they're actually congratulating themselves.

I remember the weight of the bills in my right pants pocket. As we were coming out of the bank, I asked him if he believed in blue-eyed muggers. It was a joke, but he didn't get it. Whatever he said, I don't remember. He doesn't either.

VI.

We were on the basement floor of the bank, and we took the escalator up. Escalators made me nervous. They hadn't always, I'd liked them as a kid, I'd sought them out and preferred them, but then the fear set in. I overthought the moment when I would have to pick up a foot and reactivate my slow steps before gradually accelerating. Predictably, I stumbled when I got off the escalator, and in that clumsy movement I looked back and saw that the blue-eyed man was following close behind us, along with another man whose eyes weren't blue, but brown like mine and my father's, although the two of them did look alike, maybe, I thought later; the blue-eyed mugger and the brown-eyed mugger looked a lot alike, as if they were brothers.

We turned right, heading toward Café Haití. In a fit of optimism, I thought maybe the danger would end there, and that, as on so many other occasions, my father would order an espresso and I'd get an almond frappé, and we would return the obligatory smiles of those scantily clad young women with endless legs whom I looked at with such shame and delight. But the muggers cornered us five or ten steps before we could enter the café. My father decided to do something very smart that at the same time came off as shocking or ridiculous: he decided to make a scene.

"Thieves!" he screamed, pointing at the muggers.

"You're the thieves, you fucking thugs!" shouted the brown-eyed man, pointing at us.

It sounded credible. That's what I thought in the moment—
for a thousandth of a second I thought that our accuser sounded
convincing, because the thieves were whiter than us. Or maybe
what I felt was the harsh scrutiny of the hundred or two hundred or five hundred people who were out on Paseo Ahumada and turned to look at us, alerted by the shouts.

The most brutal thing about prejudice is that if I had been
in that crowd, I would have thought we were the thieves, too.
Because of our skin color and because I was badly dressed.
The muggers were decked out in oddly colored jeans, which
were a novelty at the time, and sports shirts. I was always
badly dressed back then. Once a year my parents gave me
money for clothes, and I spent almost all of it on books, sav-
ing just a few pesos to buy a pile of used clothes, which were
usually too big or too small for me, but I didn't care. My father, on the other hand, invested in his wardrobe, but he was
and still is an eminently practical man, so he took advantage
of vacations to send his suits to the cleaners, and his weekend
clothes were all packed for the trip to La Serena. Really, I
don't remember what my father was wearing, but I tend to
think it was a sweatsuit and sneakers, or maybe that's just
how I picture it, making it up as I go.

"I don't remember what I was wearing. How could I remember something like that?" he says to me now.

He does remember this phrase:

"You stole my Ray-Bans, you fucking bum!"

That's what the blue-eyed mugger said to my father before
snatching the green, *Top Gun*–style sunglasses off his face. It
left a mark between his eyebrows. A scrape.

"I'm not the thief, it's not true!" My father's cry sounded
harrowing and naive in my ears.

It would have been easier and more logical for us to run, as if we really were the muggers, but we got caught up in a fight. It wasn't clear who exactly the aggressors were. On the corner of Ahumada and Moneda they knocked us both to the ground, and I got up quickly but saw that my dad stayed down, shouting for them to please let him look for his contact, because the blow had knocked the contact lens out of his right eye . . .

"Left."

"Okay."

. . . because the blow had knocked the contact lens out of his left eye, and that was when the blue-eyed mugger went to kick my dad while he was down but I managed to get in an awkward punch, like to his neck, and then a kick to the balls, and the blue mugger fell to the ground and I don't know where his presumed brother was—I focused on my father, who was still on all fours trying to find his lost contact, but he never found it because right at that moment a cop put him in handcuffs.

It was a civil policeman, with long hair and a striking leather jacket. All of a sudden, the whole scene had changed. The thieves had vanished, and in addition to the civil cop there were two uniformed ones who were arresting my father.

"Motherfucking cops, fucking pigs, you're taking my dad, fucking killers!"

I shouted something like that.

"I knew it would all get cleared up, I wasn't scared, but I heard you cussing out the cops and I was afraid they would arrest you and then I got worried," my dad told me later.

They led my father away in cuffs, with me following behind them and yelling, and then four or five spontaneous volunteer witnesses joined in.

"The kid is right, this man wasn't the thief, I saw the whole thing," said a woman who was around fifty years old, a street peddler, her blanket spread out and full of merchandise.

She was the one who should have been avoiding the cops, but just then she didn't seem worried about the risk, and she went with me to the gallery where the cops questioned my father. And she repeated her words several times, furiously, as if her life depended on them. And she also put her hand on my shoulder, reassured me, told me everything would be okay.

In a desperate and pathetic gesture, my father took out his wallet and brandished his credit cards at the cops.

"Now why would I need to go around robbing people?" he asked.

The cops didn't reply, just shrugged their shoulders and put it all down to a misunderstanding. They did say he could file a complaint, but my dad chose not to.

I saw the street peddler disappear into the crowd. Afterward, I walked around downtown many times looking for her. I was sure I would recognize her and I wanted to thank her, maybe, by buying whatever she was selling, but I couldn't find her.

VII.

"I never wanted to be a cop," my father clarifies. "No way. What I wanted was to join the Air Force. But that was impossible, because of my eyesight."

"Okay, I'll change that part."

"And I'd forgotten about that poem I wrote. But you left out how I used to recite."

It's true. Sometimes, at family parties, my dad would recite or more like declaim a poem—always the same, terrible
poem.

"It isn't terrible. You may not like it, but it isn't terrible. It's
a matter of personal taste."

It's a terrible poem called "The Conscript." Really, it's a
tango or a milonga that my father recited as a poem. And it
moved us. Maybe it took a few years for me to start consider-
ing it terrible.

"How come you didn't want to press charges?" As I change
the subject I feel like my question is jarring; I sound like a
journalist, or a cop.

"Because it wouldn't have made a difference, they were
never going to catch those guys."

The brief police interrogation took place just steps away
from the very optician where my father bought his contact
lenses, and where I had picked out those glasses I never wore.
All things considered, that coincidence was a good sign, according to him. We went into the store, where an elderly
man greeted my dad with the hug reserved for regular cus-
tomers.

"He wasn't elderly. He was older. Don Mauricio," my father interjects. "Still, he must be dead by now."

I wanted to tell Don Mauricio and everyone else what had
happened, but my dad squeezed my hand when I started in
on the story. He only said that he had lost his left contact and
needed a replacement ASAP. Don Mauricio promised to have
it in twenty-four hours.

We went back to Paseo Ahumada, which for a few seconds seemed like a new place to me. My father walked fast,
squinting his defenseless eye but leaning on me for support.

There was no point going to the parking garage, since he couldn't drive.

"Let's take the bus," he said.

"Let's take a taxi instead."

"A taxi to Maipú? You're crazy. Hell no."

"It's on me," I said.

He stared at me without understanding for a solid ten seconds. Only then did he remember I still had half of the money in my pocket. He still had his half too—they hadn't taken the cash. Just that pair of sunglasses.

I hailed the taxi myself, and we sat in the back with our arms around each other. I remembered another taxi ride, some years before, when we had also ridden in an embrace. My father had crashed head-on into a truck. It was the truck driver's fault, he was drunk and going the wrong way. Someone was seriously injured—one of my dad's best friends, who was riding shotgun without his seat belt. A friend who from then on was no longer his friend.

"That's not true, we still saw each other after that," my father protests, annoyed.

"But you weren't friends anymore, not such good friends."

"These things happen."

Even though it wasn't his fault, since there was an injury, my father had to spend a night in jail. My mother, my sister, and I went to pick him up, and we took the bus there but a taxi home, all four of us squeezed into the back seat. He started to talk and I don't remember his exact words, just that he was trying to reassure us, console us, but suddenly he began to cry, and then we were all crying. We cried for the rest of the trip home.

The Peugeot 404 was declared totaled. And the seat belt

mark on my father's chest stayed there for a long time. Then
he bought the Peugeot 504 that we'd parked that morning in
the Agustinas garage. During that second long taxi ride, we
didn't cry. I think it was quite the opposite: we celebrated the
episode as if we had won some kind of prize. My dad thanked
me, and over the following months he told the story to everyone he could, exaggerating it a little, as if I'd performed like
some kind of Jackie Chan or Bruce Lee.

VIII.

The first time I tried to write this story, I decided to end it
with a scene from 1994 or 1995, during my university years,
at a protest where my friends and I were running from the
cops.

"Fucking cops, motherfucking pigs, fucking killers!"

As I shouted, I remembered the cops taking my father away
in handcuffs. My feeling was ambiguous, parodic, combative,
excited, all of that at the same time. I was shouting at the cops
and remembering my dad, who figured as a victim but also a
victimizer, because he could well have been a cop, of course he
could have, at some point he'd wanted to be one.

"But I told you, I never wanted to be a cop."

"But I thought you did. When I was shouting at the cops,
I thought they were like you."

"They're like you, too."

"Maybe so. We could have been cops, we could have been
thieves."

"No, I've never stolen anything from anyone. And I never
wanted to be a cop. Fix that. You said you were going to
fix it."

I don't know if my dad would have liked to see me there, yelling at the cops.

"No, I wouldn't have liked it, but I assumed you were out there."

That ambiguous feeling never went away. At every protest, when it came time to yell at the cops, I thought of my father and felt a turbulent emotion. I felt it again the last time I was in Chile, in 2019, a few days after the October civil uprising. I traveled on short notice, alone, and I saw my parents and my extended family of dear friends. And with some of them, I went to the protests. And when people started to jump up and down and shout "El que no salta es paco" ("If you don't hop, then you're a cop"), I felt all of it again. Although this time in addition to thinking of my father I thought of my son, or felt that I was my father and was venturing into a future world where my son would protect me and defend me and judge me.

I look at photos from around that time. There's one of Silvestre smiling and wearing my glasses. He was obsessed with my glasses back then. His favorite game was to steal them off my face and run away at what was his still very slow top speed. I remember having the thought that I would recognize him in a crowd. I mean: I looked at my son's hazy, haloed face, and I asked myself if I would be able to recognize him in a crowd. And I replied, maybe to reassure myself, that I would.

IX.

"Have you finished making breakfast?" my father inter-
rupts me.

"It's ready," I say.

We sit at the table. My father, who had breakfast hours
ago, will take this moment to nibble on half a bread roll and
drink another cup of coffee.

"You'll have to start paying me royalties for everything
you've written about me," he says. "Silvestre, your dad is
writing a book about me," he says to my son.

"I wrote a book about my dad, too," says my son.

"What's it called?" my father asks.

"*Alejandro's Problems.*"

My son delays his quesadilla with chapulines so he can tell
my father all about that book. It's the anecdote of the moment, he's repeated it many times over recent days, ever more
aware of the peals of laughter it produces.

A few weeks ago, I had a fever for several days from some
strange and persistent infection that wasn't COVID, though
every half hour I became convinced that it was. One morning when I was starting to feel a little better, Silvestre insisted on staying beside me and playing COVID test, which
is still one of his recurring games. He sticks his right index
finger in his nose and looks at it in the light, theatrically, and
intones "positive" or "very positive" or "negative" or "very negative." That day, for no clear reason, he started to cry. Maybe
he felt like I was ignoring him. I asked him what was wrong,
and he leaned against my chest but didn't say anything. I
felt like it was his way of imploring me to get better once and
for all.

Then Jazmina managed to take him into the living room, and that was when he told her about his book project, *Alejandro's Problems*.

"What's your book about?" she asked him through her laughter.

"That's it, it's about all Alejandro's problems. Alejandro has a fever. Alejandro spilled a glass of water on his computer keyboard. Alejandro's scared of squirrels. Alejandro lost his glasses. Alejandro doesn't like rice pudding. Alejandro can't find his glasses because he doesn't have his glasses on. Alejandro's head hurts a lot."

Now he tells the same story to my father and adds a few more chapters. My father can't take it anymore, he's almost choking with laughter. Then he asks me if it's true about the computer. I say yes, I'd had to buy a new one. He asks if we're okay on money. Used to be, when he asked me that, I would say in a stoic voice that things were bad, thinking he would immediately transfer a little money from my inheritance. But that never happened. So now I tell him, whether it's true or not, that things are under control.

"But how could you let that happen," says my father, as though to himself.

Spilling a glass of water on the computer, I think, must seem to him like the stupidest thing that can happen to a person. But he doesn't say that.

Jazmina joins in the laughter and the breakfast, then takes Silvestre out to the kitchen garden. Some months ago, when she grew convinced that the pandemic would never end, she planted a small garden, and now she's growing chard, peas, onions, and basil. I spend five more minutes talking to my dad, about soccer. Then he says he has to go.

"I'm almost finished," I tell him.

"With what?"

"The piece I'm writing about the assault. Those paragraphs I read to you."

I want him to read the final version. I ask him to, shyly. I think he's sick of my questions, but I also sense that no, he wants to participate, he likes that I remember that story, this story.

"You want me to read it right now? You think I don't have anything else to do, that I don't have work? I'm up to my neck in work."

"I'd like it if you read it now."

"Okay," he says, unexpectedly.

I send him the file, he opens it, and for a second I think he's going to read it immediately, in front of me, that I am going to watch his face as he reads for fifteen or twenty minutes. For a second I even think that would be the natural thing to do. But he hangs up, because that is the natural thing.

I wait for his reading, his call, and I'm irrationally nervous. I don't smoke anymore, but I feel a desire to smoke one or two or all the cigarettes I can in the time it takes my father to read my story. But that would be another chapter in my son's book: Alejandro started smoking again.

"I read it," my father tells me finally, half an hour later.

"Did you like it?"

"Yes," he replies, without hesitation. "I liked it a lot, son. It's really funny."

Late Lessons in Fly-Fishing

I.

"We'll go fishing, just you and me, one of these days," my father says to my son. It's an improbable trip, but I like to imagine it: a horn honks and my son and I run out with our heavy backpacks to pile into my dad's truck—I'm not invited, but I'd love to tag along on that trip, even if only to carry the basket of sandwiches or make sure my son wears a sweater as evening approaches.

No obstacle, no challenge, no rebellion of mine would really have mattered to my father if only I had been that son he wanted: one who, for example, went fishing with him, even when teenage turbulence was raging. That son I was not, of course, would have later passed on the same passion to his own son. In our masculine family novel, my father and I would not live seven thousand kilometers away from each other, but merely a couple of towns. Perhaps the trips wouldn't be all that frequent, but at least once a year we would spend a few hours conspiring to put one over on the fish.

My father tried, of course he did. I don't remember our

first solo trip, when I was three or four years old, but he has told the story so often that it functions almost as an implanted memory. The morning of the trip, he got the idea to sit me on his knees as he pulled the car out of the garage—I can picture my little hands atop his enormous ones gripping the wheel of the Taunus, and I imagine the exuberant emotion that led me to ask him, once we were on the road, if he would also let me drive the car back into the garage when we got home that night. He promised, pleased that I liked this new game so much, but then I spent the whole trip confirming that promise, and such was my insistence that later, once we were settled in by the still waters of Peñuelas Lake, he warned me that if I kept bringing it up he would never let me drive the car in or out of the garage again. The threat worked for a while, but then I went over to play with the fish that were agonizing in a pile on the shore, and I started to invent all kinds of stories about generous silverside dads who let their silverside sons drive the car in and out of the garage over and over. Thus the whole afternoon passed.

"There was no such word as *no* for you," my dad declares every time he tells this story, which according to him exemplifies the fact that ever since I was little, my most essential personality trait has been persistence or stubbornness, though in recent years he has shifted his interpretation of the story to present it as early evidence of my literary vocation. Either way, my father always says that the word *no* didn't exist for me, while I grew up believing that for my father, the word *no* was the only one that existed.

II.

One long-ago Christmas, Santa Claus ignored our letters and decided to send us some fishing poles, with reels, lines, hooks, and all. I think my sister's excitement was genuine, although maybe it was just the obligatory politeness that was instilled in us as kids. We were children who helped set the table and greeted adults and said thank you for presents, even if the recipient of our gratitude was an abstract being like Santa.

But I was disappointed that night, and I said so. I thought that my letter, drafted excessively early and personally dispatched at the local branch of the Chilean Post Office, had been pretty clear: I wanted a BMX bike, nothing more, but nothing less. "Maybe next year," my mother soothed me with nervous sweetness. That was when, of course, at the age of eight, I began to understand the sophisticated Christmas hoax.

We spent that Christmas Eve with the neighbors, enduring the tantrum of a little girl who bawled her eyes out because she had received a doll that didn't cry. What I mean is, she had received a doll that in theory was supposed to cry, but it didn't work, and so its owner cried instead. It was a technical flaw, it could be fixed, her desperate parents said. I tried to console her by telling her how I hated fishing, and yet I'd gotten a fishing pole for Christmas. The girl went right on crying with even more heartrending sadness, in solidarity with me.

It's not true that I hated to fish. I liked the beach better, but I still had a good time at the Lo Ovalle reservoir near Casablanca, which was our most frequent destination; I es-

pecially liked the exciting ritual of pounding the stakes of
our orange tent into the earth. They were always two- or
three-day trips that my mother spent listening to cassettes by
Adamo and Puma Rodríguez while paging for the umpteenth time through some copies of *Vea* magazine at a prudent distance from the relentless sun, though occasionally she
put on a straw hat and a pair of giant sunglasses to sit beside
my father as he whiled away the hours absorbed in his favorite hobby.

My sister and I went over to them every once in a while,
maybe just to be sure we were still visible. My father answered
my questions with a faint, friendly smile in a distracted, hushed
tone, as if he had forgotten his characteristic booming voice
back in Santiago. More than the volume of his voice, it was
his stillness and patience that disconcerted me. He barely even
changed position: when he got tired of his blue folding chair,
he'd find a spot on a rock somewhere. But most often he
would be on his feet, then crouch down for a long time, then
stand back up for another long time.

I'm sure that back then I wasn't actually fixated on watching my dad, which I would have found terribly boring. Who
knows what those days were really like. I remember how I'd
lie out in the sun on the shore of the reservoir, my left hand
pressed against my chest, until I achieved the coveted inverse
tattoo. And how my sister and I would play with Andrea, a
charming and beautiful girl with a cleft lip, a little younger
than me, who lived there year-round because she was the
daughter of Juanito Plaza, the campground manager. The three
of us would go swimming or rowing or defying the rats as we
leapt between rocks, terrified and joyful. We also used to pre-

tend that one of us was a foreigner who drove up in an imaginary Jeep and spoke an incomprehensible language, and the others were locals who taught the newcomer about the language and customs of the town. My sister liked to make me say cuss words, which in that fantasyland were just common, everyday words. *Huevón*, for example, in that country, didn't mean *asshole*, but rather *Have a nice day, friend*.

III.

My sister preferred to fish with a line, while I would settle in with my rod to imitate my father's movements. Even with all his fisherman's patience, though, he could barely tolerate our display of ineptitude and blunders. He taught us all his tricks, tried to help us refine our technique, and avoided chastising us at all costs, but after five failed attempts, which were maybe actually twenty (or thirty), he couldn't hide his irritation. Then my sister would go back to Andrea and I would sneak away to find a solitary spot where I could fish my own way.

At night, I would show my dad the few fish that I'd managed to catch in spite of my technical deficiencies. His congratulations were exaggerated and affectionate.

"Why didn't you stay with me?"

"Because the fish I was looking for were somewhere else."

That was my answer one hot night we spent playing dominos, with the pieces set up on the ground like little tin soldiers.

"Stay and fish with me," he would often urge. "And if you get bored you can go play for a while, but then come back."

One morning we woke up to news of a school of fish. I ran

off to the water with my rod, and all I had to do was cast and catch—sometimes there was a pair of shining silversides on a single hook. I spent two or three hours toiling away with childish greed at that millionaire pond. Stick a bloodworm on the hook, pound a nail through the gills and wounded mouths of moribund fish to add them to the line that I would later drag euphorically back to the tent at a triumphant march; over the years I've become squeamish, and now it's hard to accept how many times I repeated these actions.

When he'd heard about the school, my father had decided to spend the afternoon walking with my mom and having a few beers with Andrea's dad. I asked him why that day, when it was so easy, he had decided not to fish.

"That's exactly why," he said. "Because it was too easy, there's no fun in it."

IV.

"Your dad was my dad that summer," says Cristián, a dear friend from adolescence I fell out of touch with decades ago. We've just reunited, or really we haven't seen each other yet: for days, we've been exchanging long voice messages with the promise to meet up again as soon as possible.

In the days Cristián is talking about, he and I spent our time seeking out remedies for acne, which was abusing his reddish skin and my brown skin with equal cruelty. Cristián heard that you could combat zits with aloe vera masks, so as soon as evening fell we set off in search of a plant, then locked ourselves in my room to coat our faces with its pulp. It all happened in secret and darkness, like some sort of drug deal.

It was my dad who, unexpectedly, invited Cristián to spend summer vacation with us.

"Where's your backpack, Cristián?" my father asked him.

"What backpack?"

My dad gave a laugh and then called Gina, Cristián's mom, to ask permission, and my friend went running home. He came back fifteen minutes later with an express camping backpack that we squeezed into the car's overcrowded trunk.

"I remember we listened to Simon & Garfunkel the whole way there," Cristián tells me. "And that your mom kept turning up the volume and your dad would turn it down. And that she drove faster than he did."

"And do you remember the tea sandwiches?"

"No," says Cristián.

We'd brought some blackberry jam on bread for the road, and my mom had gotten the idea to call them "tea sandwiches" so they would seem fancier. It was one of those off-hand jokes that stick in your memory as if they held some kind of significance.

Five hours later and we were sprawled in the living room of a cold house in La Serena. I feel like I should remember that trip better, but I oversimplify it—I imagine we spent that couple of weeks in February playing paddle ball on the beach or nursing illegal beers in a dance club in Coquimbo while we speculated on sensational, imminent romances. Cristián remembers it differently. He remembers, for example, that one morning we looked through my binoculars and saw, out past the rocks of a deserted beach, two women swimming naked in the ocean.

"I don't know how you could forget something like that,"

Cristián tells me, rightly. "The northern goddesses, we called them."

The phrase *northern goddesses* triggers a memory in me, or maybe just the desire to remember. Both of us, however, clearly recall my father clowning around on the streets of La Serena. His favorite prank was to greet some stranger as if he knew them, approaching effusively and giving exaggerated hugs. And when the stranger said there'd been a mistake, my dad fell all over himself in apologies, and then came out with his triumphant phrase:

"Well, the physical resemblance is frankly uncanny."

Cristián and I were supporting accomplices, barely able to contain our laughter. Just when we seemed about to get bored with the joke, my dad went up to a kid about ten years old and greeted him with extra excitement, pretending it was a reunion with his best friend's son.

"I can't believe how big you've gotten, Pepito Roblero! I would love to see your dad again!"

Disconcerted, the boy clarified that he was not Pepito Roblero. My dad apologized, gave his trademark phrase, and we went on whiling away the afternoon with our ice cream cones. Maybe half an hour later, we ran into the same kid again near La Recova, and my dad again lunged at him to tell him, euphorically:

"Pepito Roblero, we just saw a kid who looks exactly like you!"

That wasn't how my dad usually acted, I know that for sure. But Cristián claims my dad was indeed always like that.

"He was really nice. And so welcoming to me. Always cracking jokes, just like you."

"I don't think so."

"Well, it's only natural you don't want to think you're like your dad. Back then I thought the two of you were similar. But we never learn to really see our parents well. Who was it who wrote that, again?"

I'm late in realizing I'm the one who wrote that. I'm happy to learn that Cristián read a book of mine. We talk about that. He still knows some of my teenage poems by heart. They are terrible poems, which I would like him to forget immediately. He affectionately disagrees.

"We went to the plaza several times, the three of us, and your dad always did the same thing."

"It wasn't just once?"

"No! It was many times. Maybe I'm the one who should have become a writer."

"Definitely! And what did my mom and my sister do? The way I remember it, you and I were always together and my sister and my mom were always together and my dad was always alone."

"Your mom and your sister spent the whole day at the beach. But as I remember it, you and I were always around your dad."

"Really? I thought my dad was always off fishing, and you and I wandered around aimlessly."

"Yeah, but we also went with him to Punta de Choros, and to other beaches," says Cristián.

My friend's memories awaken in me the sleeping image of the immense, semideserted beach at Punta de Choros. I see myself and Cristián looking for clams along the beach, digging in our heels and twisting, dying with laughter at our clumsy dance steps while my dad, wearing the fluorescent suit of an expert fisherman, slowly waded out into the water.

"Was that the beach where we saw the northern god-desses?" I ask.

"I don't know," he says. "But after that I kept seeing them everywhere, they were like ghosts."

"Really?"

"No."

V.

A couple of years after that trip Cristián remembers so well, a work friend invited my dad to Río Pescado, near Puerto Varas. That's when he discovered fly-fishing, which then became his main and perhaps definitive passion. We were still living under the same roof when he started taking trips to the south to fish in the Puelo or Baker rivers, and later he and my mom spent several summers in Villa La Angostura, near Bariloche: it was a long trip in the truck, with stops in Temuco and Osorno before crossing into Argentina. As I understand it, at some point my mom tried to join in his fly-fishing fever, though she spent most of her time on those trips reading novels, a hobby that was new to her then and that she has never renounced.

Several years later, when I was working as a literary critic, every time I reviewed a novel negatively, my mother went and read that book and liked it. Of course, I also wrote favorable reviews—they were in fact more common—but the books I celebrated didn't seem to interest her at all. In any case, I liked writing for the newspaper that my mother read. And I enjoyed talking to her about those books, though our conversations had a tinge of friendly reproach. ("I don't write for the critics, I write for the critics' mothers," the author Hernán Rivera Letelier once said, as though sensing this imbalance I'm talking about. It is truly a magnificent sentence.)

VI.

My father and I never talked about books. That's why I was so surprised when, some ten years ago, he handed me his copy of *Nada es para siempre*, by Norman Maclean, and asked me to read it.

"You're going to love it," he said. "It's my favorite book."

The fact that my father even had a favorite book was news to me—news that I didn't take too seriously. Plus, I thought that title reeked of self-help, and so did the cover image, a still from the Robert Redford movie, though I only learned its provenance months later as I was organizing the small, spontaneous towers of my to-read pile. That's when I learned that the original title of Maclean's book, and of the movie in English, was *A River Runs Through It*. I confirmed online that *Nada es para siempre*, or "Nothing lasts forever," was the commercial title of the movie in Spanish, and also that critics considered Maclean's book to be a classic of US literature.

Not even the certainty that *A River Runs Through It* was, in theory, good literature made me want to read it. I do remember, though, that later on I pondered that gesture of my father's with curiosity. Why, instead of giving me the book for my birthday or for Christmas, had he *lent* me his copy? Maybe he wasn't immune to literary fetishism; maybe he wanted me to read every one of the pages he had read and all the words he'd underlined—because some sections of the book were underlined, which also, somehow, surprised me.

More or less around that time, I read *How I Came to Know Fish*, by Ota Pavel, which my dad would love, and *Trout Fishing in America* by Richard Brautigan, which he would find weird, but it didn't even occur to me to mention those books to him.

For a long time, maybe two years, my father kept asking if I had read his favorite book yet, and I would reply that I had it on my nightstand and would read it any day now, and he would ask me again to please take care of it, not to lose it, which was in a way unnecessary, because he knew I took care of books. I was the bookish one, after all; I took care of books just as scrupulously as he cared for his pool cues and his sophisticated fishing implements, including the flies he used to jealously make himself, staying up till midnight lit by a small, powerful lamp that he'd placed on a corner of his desk specifically for those nights of obsessive craftwork.

VII.

"Can I stop by?" my dad asked one morning, over the phone. "I'm five minutes from your house."

It was a Friday, and I wasn't expecting him. We drank coffee and talked, about what, I don't remember. It was unusual to have him in my house, and I liked it.

"Really, I came to get my book," he said, when in theory he was on his way out.

He started to scour my shelves himself, like when I was a teenager and he would lose something and barge into my room to search my closet, and I would worry about him finding my pot or my diaries. I joined in the search for the book, a little nervous, but after a while I promised I would look for it properly and return it to him as soon as possible. I gave a sigh of relief when my father left.

Later that day, I resumed the search. I was sure I had relegated Maclean to the shelves closest to the floor, dangerously near the pile of books that I would occasionally give away—when I was invited to speak at a school, for example, I would take books from that pile and donate them a little guiltily, aware that it was meaningless to give someone what you yourself disdained. Terribly ashamed, I concluded that I had unwittingly donated the very book my father had so often asked me to take care of. I tried to buy it, but his was an old copy, and in any case there was the matter of the underlined sentences. Nor did I look for it all that hard, to be honest.

"I can't find it, Dad," I had to admit a couple weeks later, at my mom's birthday party, I think. "But I'm sure I have it. Plus, I want to read it."

"Come on, I know you don't want to read it," said my father with unexpected jollity, as if it were totally unimportant. "You don't want to read it because I'm the one who recommended it."

"You could at least tell him you read it, lie to him," my mother interrupted. "It's a book about fishing, your dad is really interested in fishing."

Her urging me to lie was already strange enough, but that second sentence was even stranger, because of course there was no need for her to inform me of my father's interest in fishing.

"I didn't read it, but the movie is really good," said my sister. "It's one of Brad Pitt's first roles."

"The book is better," my father declared.

"I want to read it when Alejandro gives it back. You should

watch it, Ale, it even won an Oscar. But you never watch the movies that win Oscars."

"Sometimes I do," I said. "Did you guys see *Brokeback Mountain*? I think that won an Oscar, or a few of them. And it's about fishing, too. I think in Spanish it's called . . ."

"*Secreto en la montaña* . . . Of course we did, Alejandro, everyone saw that movie," my dad said.

"It's really good," said my mom.

"Did you read the story by Annie Proulx?"

"It's based on a story? I didn't know that," said my dad.

We were at the patio table devouring what was left of a barbecue. The conversation trailed off for a few seconds, as if we were passing through a tunnel that was short but long enough to make the silence clear. But then we started talking about *Brokeback Mountain* again. My dad said that among fishermen it was common to make jokes about that movie. I asked him if any of those friends were gay.

"Who knows," he replied. "Not that I'm aware of."

Since the question didn't seem to make him the slightest bit uncomfortable, I started talking superciliously about how much it would bother me to learn that he still made fun of gay people. He replied angrily that he had never made fun of gay people. He demanded I come up with a single memory I had of him being homophobic. And it's true that I've never heard him make a homophobic comment. I had to admit he was right.

"So then what do you laugh about with your fishermen friends?"

"Please, they're jokes, son. Don't lose your sense of humor. It's the best thing about you."

My mother and sister nodded. I picked up the guitar and

started to sing. That had always been my strategy with them when I wanted to change the subject.

VIII.

"And you really never read the book?" asks Silvia, my publisher, when I tell her this story.

"Never," I say.

She looks at me, incredulous and I even think disappointed. We're on the train from Madrid to Barcelona, and we've been talking for a couple of hours now about this essay, among other things. She goes quiet for maybe a couple of quick kilometers.

"If I were you I'd read that book, Alejandro. It's the only way for you to finish the piece."

"But maybe it's better to leave it open, unfinished," I say.

"Do you really not care about what your dad wanted to tell you? Does he still ask you if you read the book?"

"No. I think he assumes I'm never going to read it."

"And he's disappointed," says Silvia.

"Or he forgot about it," I reply. "It's the world in reverse," I tell her then, redundantly. "I'm supposed to be the one who reads and recommends books. And he's the one who refuses to read them."

Silvia lowers her voice, or rather tunes in to the right tone or rhythm in which to talk about her own memories. How, at four years old, she was the only one in her family who went with her father to fish in the rivers of the Pyrenees. "I became a fisherman out of necessity," her dad used to say, and he sneered at the little green vests worn by those upstart sport fishermen, because as a child he had fished in order to eat.

Silvia remembers how on those excursions her father would leave her sitting on the bank alone, momentarily concentrated on the birds or the whirl of the water. Then the feeling of waiting would grow and anxiety set in, but she still felt safe: she knew her father would come back any minute.

"He doesn't remember any of that now," Silvia tells me.

"He forgot?"

"He forgot everything," she says. "Alzheimer's. I have to introduce my boyfriend to him every time we visit."

"Does he approve of him?"

"Yes," she says, with a broad smile that I recognize, but that also seems, suddenly, new. "Every time I introduce them, my dad likes him."

IX.

My last day in Barcelona, I ask for Maclean's book at several bookstores, with no luck. In Spain it's called *El río de la vida*, "The River of Life," a beautiful and sober title, and it came out twelve years ago with Libros del Asteroide, a press whose catalog I adore. If my dad had lent me that edition, this story would be completely different. I feel snobbish, uncomfortable, silly.

Silvia's story makes me remember the last trip we took, just my dad and me, when I was sixteen years old; he had already contracted his incurable passion for fly-fishing, and I for literature. By that point we didn't get along well, and we both had a hard time hiding it. The trip was long and perhaps mistimed, and maybe responded to the desire to find each other again, to get closer.

We headed in from Linares toward the mountains until

we found a good place to pitch the same tent as always on the shore of the Achibueno River. My dad conscientiously studied the landscape, waiting a long time until the sun was less intense ("The trout are just waking up from their nap," he said at some point), before disappearing upriver.

I sank into whatever long novel I was reading at the time, though every once in a while I would pause, distracted by the silvered opacity of the canelo trees and the spectacle of the diaphanous sky and the slow, crystalline water, while I remembered those lines by Neruda I had recently discovered: "I must speak of the ground that the stones darken / of the river that, though enduring, destroys itself."

Then, maybe an hour later, I missed my father. It was strange. It's not that I thought he might be lost or in danger, but I saw myself there, alone like some kind of wayward tourist, without even a pair of powerful sneakers to put on to go look for him, to help him. It only lasted a few minutes, and then he came back.

"How's it going?" I asked.

"Good," he said.

He showed me the photo he had just taken with his brand-new and, at that time, revolutionary digital camera. My father was holding a trout barely bigger than his hand, but the most striking thing about the image was his serious, inscrutable pose. Immediately after taking that photo—an artisanal selfie, so to speak—he had returned the trout to the river. By then he already threw the fish he caught back in the water, he didn't even keep the minimum allowed.

"What page are you on?" he asked me.

I don't remember what I said. Page 150, for example.

"I'll be back in forty pages," he said then, playfully.

At sundown we cooked up some noodles, and then I kept my nose buried in the novel, freezing cold but well lit and perhaps a little warmed by a bright kerosene lamp. I went to sleep very late and woke up in broad daylight and terrified by an enormous boar that, after having eaten all our sandwiches, was trying to get into the tent—I suppose so it could eat me next. My dad, who had left at dawn, came back a while later in search of a nonexistent breakfast. We decided to stay anyway, meting out some oranges and sliced bread that we had fortuitously left in the truck.

At some point in the afternoon, I went out with my dad and took some photos of him. I had seen him practicing those comical, choreographed fly-fishing casts before, not in a river, but standing in the cramped front yard of our house. Now, watching him balance on some rocks, I better understood the relationship between that technical challenge and the obsessive effort to decipher the water's course. For just a few moments I was able to glimpse a heroic, romantic scene. I thought of that sudden, intrusive immersion in nature, the recovery of a desire, so often put off or stifled, to belong to that strange and captivating landscape. And then it all went back to seeming childish: a serious man imitating the tempting movements of some hypothetical, distracted insects. The crazed baton of an orchestra director intent on making inaudible music.

But what I best understood was that desire to defy the chronometer. The experience of fishing functioned in a decidedly similar way to literature. For those couple of days, our languages coexisted. What I mean is: we coexisted, it worked. And when we got back home and my mom asked how the trip had been and we both replied that we'd had a great time, neither of us was lying.

X.

"Your dad was my dad that summer," Cristián says again in another voice message, as though slipping me that important phrase on the sly, so I'll go on writing this essay that he doesn't know I'm writing.

My father was other people's father many times, in moments of strife: they would ask to talk to him and he'd receive them right away, and I would usually listen as they described their conundrums, which were academic, work related, professional, or even religious. But that often happens with fathers: they become father figures for everyone except their own children. The very expression *father figure* is more common in plural, while when you talk about a *mother figure* it tends to allude to someone who has substituted a lost mother. Maybe it's true when they say that *you only have one mother*, although my own son, who already knows kids with two moms (and kids with two dads), would beg to differ.

"Did you say hi to your parents for me?" Cristián asks.

"Yes," I reply. "My dad was really happy that you remember him."

I haven't actually said anything to them, but I lie in order to force myself to annul the lie immediately: as soon as we hang up, I call my parents to talk to them about Cristián.

"He was the nicest of all your friends," says my dad.

My mother's head appears in the frame and nods, but she doesn't want to establish hierarchies. As they finish dinner, the two of them remember Hugo, Mario, Maricel, Carla, and Angélica. They remember all of them.

"Villablanca, that was Cristián's last name, right?"

"Yep."

"And is he still so happy?"

"Yes," I say, pleased to be telling the truth.

XI.

"Your word, that word you love so much!" says my son one afternoon, furious.

"Which one? What word?"

"You know what word, 'cause you like it a lot, you love it, you would kiss that word!"

Of course I knew which one. I, once a child who believed there was no such thing as *no*, was now in love with the word, according to my son. Silvestre had not been such a reckless child, but for weeks he'd been clambering up onto furniture and trying to climb bookshelves, and he had just discovered he could reach the knife drawer (which, as such, immediately ceased to be the knife drawer). I had no choice but to regularly resort to the word *no*.

As he scolded me, my mind wandered to the image of myself at three or four years old, I presume with fewer words than him, although, according to the official version, I had enough to invent pasts and futures for those poor fish who were so addicted to butterworms. When Silvestre calmed down, or rather got bored with complaining, it seemed pointless to go back over the same explanation as always, which by that point was understood, so I picked him up and patted his hair, which was miraculously long or almost long. (One of my greatest aspirations as a child was to be allowed to grow my hair long, but he likes to go to the barber, though maybe what he really likes is to sit in the chair and tell the barber, with the authority of those in the know: "Like Paul McCartney from the Beatles, please.")

"I'm never going to say the word *no* to you again," I promised my son. "From now on, when you're in a situation I think is dangerous, we're going to replace the word *no* with the word *ne*."

He loved the idea, which mysteriously worked for several months that were terrific, because our agreement granted me a sort of superpower. Whenever it was necessary, I simply got close to his ear and said in an exaggeratedly low voice:

"Son, *ne*."

Silvestre not only obeyed, but he did so with a smile. Other family members went on using the tyrannical and biblical *no*, with predictably terrible results. The warm empire of the word *ne* began to crumble, sadly, when Silvestre's teacher told us there was a little girl in his class who hit him, and instead of asking or demanding that she stop, he would kindly and gently say *ne*, so that the girl went right on hitting him.

Silvestre and I still use the word *ne*, jokingly, almost as a reminder of a past language. Or maybe it's the same language in constant transformation, although always linked to music and stories and always full of imitations, jokes, and tongue twisters. I still do my best to disguise obligatory things behind little games that bring out the adventurous side of brushing teeth or bathing or getting dressed by himself. It's much harder for me to rush him every morning to go to school, maybe because I myself have never managed to fully acquiesce to chronological time—I've always been the sort who would rather stick around and talk. He doesn't like to be rushed, but who does? And who likes to be reminded all the time that life is not a game? We were all once professionals of playing; the obsession with writing has been, for me, a way of prolonging the game as long as I can.

My son is asleep, and I lie down beside him to read *A River Runs Through It* while I think about the enormous quantity of books and songs that in the future I will recommend to him and he will ignore in favor of something else. I like Maclean's book. It's such a familiar and foreign world; that is, it's similar to a world I simultaneously inhabited and rejected. That violence that is so masculine, that brotherhood, so masculine, that lack of communication, so very masculine.

There are many technical passages about fly-fishing, and I make an effort to understand and assimilate them, as if I were reading a manual on the eve of a trip. And of course I see my father practicing his choreographies, or at the corner of his desk working away at his flies. He once explained to me something that is also explained in the book: that when you make a fly, the idea is not to imitate insects as we see them, but rather the way they would look at water level, or how a fish would see them from below.

I'm reading the ebook in English, but at times I pause to mentally translate phrases, and I picture the paperback that my father read eagerly and even underlined, and later wanted to share with me. And as I translate, I get carried away by the easy and illusory thought that I'm translating my father for the first time. "The cast is so soft and slow that it can be followed like an ash settling from a fireplace chimney," says Maclean, paving the way for this sentence: "One of life's quiet excitements is to stand somewhat apart from yourself and watch yourself softly becoming the author of something beautiful, even if it is only a floating ash." Yes, Dad. That is exactly what writing is to me.

"Poets talk about 'spots of time,' but it is really fishermen who experience eternity compressed into a moment," writes Maclean, adding: "No one can tell what a spot of time is until suddenly the whole world is a fish and the fish is gone." I imagine my father reading these words and thinking about the unfortunate irony of having a poet-ish son who remained immune to the beauty of fishing.

Although millions of readers have turned its pages, *A River Runs Through It*, for a moment, is a book that only my father and I know. I am sure that he also underlined this sentence: "It is those we live with and love and should know who elude us."

XII.

"I finally read the book."

"What book?"

"The one with the movie, *Nada es para siempre*."

"The one I lent you and you never returned?"

"Right."

"I thought you'd lost it."

"I didn't lose it. I brought it to Mexico. I'll bring it to you when I come to Chile."

"Can you read me the dedication? It's really nice."

"I don't have it right now."

"Go find it, I'll wait."

I look for the dedication on my Kobo, and I translate it for my dad, but he clarifies that he doesn't mean the author's dedication, but the one that his friends wrote by hand on the first page. Now I think I remember that there was, in fact, a handwritten dedication on the book's first page.

"I don't see it," I tell him, clumsily.

"You don't see it because you don't have the book," he tells me, holding back laughter. "I have it."

I realize that he knows I'm lying, but it takes a minute to clarify the situation, until he confesses that he took the lost copy from my living room himself.

So, that morning when he came to my house unannounced and searched my shelves, my father did find the book. It could only have been that day, I think. I ask him, and he confirms it. I read him some passages from this very essay. He splits his sides laughing.

"It was my little revenge," he tells me in the exact tone of someone confessing to a prank.

I laugh. I remember the conversation a few pages back, a few days back. I sense that my mother and sister also know about this little revenge. I ask why he let the joke go on for so long. So many years.

"Because I forgot," he says.

I don't believe him. I think he did want to teach me a lesson. Or that it really was important to him for me to read that book.

"I liked it a lot, anyway," I tell him. "And I'm sorry I didn't read it when you wanted me to."

"That's great!" he says with genuine enthusiasm. "I knew you'd like it. Did you watch the movie?"

"Not yet, but I'm going to."

"Don't watch it, the book is better."

"How come the book is better?" I feel ridiculous asking a question like that.

"I watched the movie first, and the images are spectacular. But the book feels more real. The characters, especially. You can give the characters whatever faces you want. The book feels more like your own. You can identify with it."

I tell him that I'm writing about those fishing trips from my childhood. And about his invitation to Silvestre a couple of weeks ago.

"I always assume you're writing about something," he says after a nearly long silence. "All the time, your whole life, you've been writing about something, Alejandro." His words sound affectionate and condescending at the same time.

We talk about fly-fishing, and I don't want to take notes, though suddenly it seems that my father, like a professor, is emphasizing certain phrases so that I'll register and remember them. My attention wanders, but those emphases bring me back to the conversation.

"It's just that you never stop learning," he says, for example. "Never. A fly fisherman, even the most expert one, never stops learning."

"Is that what you wanted to tell me?" I ask him.

"What?"

"That we never stop learning."

"What do you mean?"

"When you asked me to read that book."

"I think you already knew. We all know that, there's no need to read it in a book."

"But I learned it from books."

"No, you didn't learn it from books. And I was talking about fly-fishing."

"But why did you keep telling me to read that book?"

"Because I liked it!"

"Me too."

"You're right," he admits after a few seconds. "I did want to tell you something. I wanted you to read it so I could tell you something. But it was such a long time ago. I'm sure that over these years I've already told you some other way."

"I know," I tell him. "We're able to talk to each other now."

"We've always been able to talk."

"We talk better now."

"Yes. Hey, I need to go. But first tell me, son, do you want the three of us to go fishing, with Silvestre?"

"But we're really far away," I reply, surprised.

"It doesn't have to be right now. Silvestre will have a great time. And I can teach you both how to fish. It could be next year, or the year after. There's time."

"Of course there's time, Dad," I tell him. "Let's do it."

Message to
My Son

You're on the sofa, two steps away from me, reading on your own. It's a new and for now sporadic habit: you sound each syllable out until you manage to form the words, to discover them in their entirety. After one or two complete sentences, you usually interrupt your solitary reading to share your findings with me. But sometimes you'll keep going, and instead of talking to me you'll laugh, or repeat certain unknown words that are like flashes of music, candidates for being burned into your memory.

Reading to yourself: it's odd that we use this metaphorical expression to allude to silent reading. In reality there's no such thing as silent reading: reading has a built-in voice included in the seeming silence, a voice that the silence can't destroy. For now, your reading to yourself is audible. And that murmur, that stammer, that joyful sounding out—sometimes it sounds like a secret. Of course it does: to read is to receive secrets, but also to tell secrets to oneself.

I've thought before about that solitude of reading. So noisy and yet so different from noise. So silent and so different from silence. And then there's that other, more problematic silence of the person who is with a reader. In theory, we readers are the ideal accomplices for other readers, but sometimes we want or have to—or we feel that we have to—interrupt other people's reading, and we become, if only momentarily, those awful people who barge in with the news that the electricity bill must be paid or the dishes washed. As a teenager, I used books as shields. They were weapons that allowed me to surround myself with an inaccessible domain. And I remember reading, or pretending to read, just to keep others from talking to me.

I'm in the armchair, two steps away from you, rereading to myself (in silence) the penultimate version of this book while I listen to you read to yourself (aloud) a children's novel by Juan Villoro, and for a few seconds I foster the growing sense that the words coming out of your mouth are the same as the ones in front of me. It takes me a while to imagine that day in the future imperfect when you will read this book. It's not the first time I've imagined it, of course; I have pictured that day incessantly. The idea that you will read, that you are reading this book right now, sometimes brings me overwhelming joy, and other times an emotion much more difficult to define.

"Dad, I want to sleep with you tonight, in Mom's bed," you tell me now, while I try to brush your teeth.

"Mom's bed is my bed, too."

"No, it's Mom's."

"Then where's my bed?"

"You don't have one," you tell me, laughing.

My plans for the evening were to watch a movie and maybe even fall asleep with the TV on, the way I often did back in the Stone Age, but I can't figure out a way to refuse your request.

"Look, Dad, I put on the PJs Mom likes," you tell me.

"Do you miss her?"

"I don't miss her or mister her, but I like to wear her favorite PJs."

You miss your mother and you deal with it in your own way. Her absence is neither frequent nor unusual, but this trip has been a long one for you. I think that, like me, you feel the days when the family is incomplete to be like the inverse of a trip. And that when your mom or I return, it's as if all three of us were returning. Last night, after spending five days in Buenos Aires, your mom landed in Santiago. It's the first time we have ever switched countries. The fact that she is now in Chile while I'm here in Mexico reinforces for me the warm illusion that we live there and you and I are the ones who are traveling, here to visit, I don't know, maybe the Teotihuacán pyramids.

I read you your stories, sing your three or four songs, and you fall asleep in your mom's bed. I go to the living room to finish reading the penultimate version of this book. And I think again about that future person who you are right now, and I imagine that you read, that you are reading this book, and you like it or don't, you enjoy it or get bored, you are moved or indifferent.

"My dad is never serious. And the only time he said something serious, everyone laughed," you often tell your friends. I like to think that I will always have the ability to make you laugh.

I don't even know if I want you to read this book. It's not necessary, of course. It exists thanks to you and you are its main recipient, but I wrote it, above all, to accompany, with my friends, the mysteries of happiness. It's okay if you don't read it.

"When you get old, I'm going to buy you the best wheelchair so we can go on walks," you told me when you had just turned four years old. I would rather tell you every one of these stories, expanded and improved, someday in your youth when you are bored enough to take me out for a walk in that splendid wheelchair you promised me. I like to think that this book is nothing but a script for those slow outings of the future.

MEXICO CITY
January 31, 2023

Acknowledgments

The supportive and complicit eye of my friend Andrés Braithwaite was key to finding a shape for this book. I don't think there are any synonyms, Andrés, for this phrase: thank you.

I am also grateful for the constant and good-humored company of Silvia Sesé, and the generosity of Megan McDowell, who translated early versions of several of these pieces in English, which were later edited by Sheila Glaser (from *The New York Times Magazine*), Daniel Gumbiner (*McSweeney's Quarterly*), and Deborah Treisman (*The New Yorker*). Commentary from Jacques Testard, Lindsey Schwoeri, Camille LeBlanc, Lorena Bou, Elda Cantú, Lorena Fuentes, and Andrea Palet was also important to me. And special thanks to Teresa Velázquez and Horacio Zambra, meticulous landscapers of the family tree.

Many friends—the usual ones, plus a few new ones and others who were miraculously recovered—made valuable comments about the whole book or some of its parts. I list them here in curious alphabetical promiscuity: Andrés Anwandter, Sebastián Aracena, Marina Azahua, Felipe Bianchi, Fabrizio Copano, Alejandra Costamagna, Mauricio Durán, Elizabeth Duval, Daniela Escobar, Andrés Florit, Emilio Hinojosa, Luke

Ingram, Juanito Mellado, Rodrigo Rojas, Daniel Saldaña, Juan Santander Leal, César Tejeda, Alejandra Torres, Antonia Torres, Vicente Undurraga, Miguel Vélez, Cristián Villablanca, and Isabel Zapata.

Jazmina and Silvestre are the true authors of this book, and I've spent several hours now trying for a rational sentence, the kind with subject and predicate, that measures up to my gratitude, but I need to go because Silvestre gets out of school at one thirty—I like to arrive fifteen or twenty minutes before they open the doors and he runs to hug me like someone returning from a lengthy trip through deserts and across savannas.